Love's True Promise

Christian romance fiction, Volume 7

Angela Marie Stewart

Published by B&H Publishing Group, 2024.

LOVE'S TRUE PROMISE

First edition. September 5, 2024.

Copyright © 2024 Angela Marie Stewart.

ISBN: 979-8227034175

Written by Angela Marie Stewart.

Table of Contents

To those who believe in the power of love and the strength of faith.

For the dreamers who trust in God's timing, the warriors who face life's trials with grace, and the hearts that hold onto hope when the road seems uncertain.

This book is for you.

May your love story be a reflection of His divine promise, and may you always find joy in the journey.

Chapter 1: The Promise of Love

The morning sun cast a golden hue over the small town of Pinebrook, its rays gently illuminating the rows of white picket fences and neatly trimmed lawns. The air was crisp and clean, filled with the scent of blooming flowers and the distant hum of life beginning to stir. Birds sang in the trees, their melodies weaving a symphony that echoed through the quiet streets, heralding the promise of a new day.

Among the quaint houses that lined Maple Street, one stood out, not because of its size or grandeur, but because of the warmth that seemed to emanate from within. The modest two-story home, with its ivy-clad walls and flower-filled window boxes, was the residence of Grace Elliott, a woman whose life had been marked by both trials and triumphs. Yet, through it all, she had clung to the belief that true love was not only possible but divinely ordained.

Grace was in her late twenties, with soft brown hair that fell in loose waves around her shoulders and eyes that sparkled with a quiet determination. Her smile was kind and welcoming, the kind that could light up a room and put anyone at ease. She had a heart that loved deeply and a spirit that sought to serve others, always putting their needs before her own. Her faith was the cornerstone of her life, guiding her decisions and giving her strength in times of uncertainty.

As the morning light filtered through the lace curtains of her bedroom, Grace rose from her bed, her mind already turning to the day ahead. She had always been an early riser, finding solace in the stillness of the morning, when the world was just beginning to wake. It was during these quiet moments that she spent time in prayer, seeking guidance from the One who had never failed her.

She knelt by the side of her bed, her hands clasped together, and closed her eyes. The words of 1 Corinthians 13:13 echoed in her mind: "And now these three remain: faith, hope and love. But the greatest of these is love." She had always believed that love was the greatest gift of all, a gift that came from God and was meant to be shared. It was a promise she had made to herself long ago, a promise to love deeply, fully, and without reservation.

Grace's thoughts drifted to the person who had always been in her heart, though their paths had not crossed in years. Ethan Matthews had been her best friend since childhood, a boy with a heart as big as his dreams. They had grown up together, shared secrets, and made countless memories that had shaped who they were. But as they reached adulthood, life had taken them in different directions. Ethan had left Pinebrook to pursue his career as a doctor in a big city, while Grace had remained, dedicating her life to helping those in her community.

Despite the distance, Grace had never forgotten the promise they had made to each other on the night before Ethan left. It was a promise born of friendship and love, a vow to always be there for one another, no matter where life took them. "No matter what happens, Grace, I promise I'll always come back to you," Ethan had said, his voice filled with sincerity. And Grace, with tears in her eyes, had made the same promise.

Years had passed since that night, and though their lives had taken different paths, the promise remained etched in Grace's heart. She believed that God had a plan for both of them, a plan that would bring them back together when the time was right. It was this belief that gave her hope and the strength to continue loving Ethan from afar.

As she finished her prayer, Grace rose from her knees, feeling a sense of peace wash over her. Today was a special day, the day that would mark the beginning of a new chapter in her life. She had received a letter from Ethan a few weeks ago, a letter that had stirred emotions she thought she had long buried. He was coming back to Pinebrook, and he wanted to see her.

The news had filled Grace with a mixture of excitement and trepidation. What would it be like to see Ethan again after all these years? Would the bond they had shared still be as strong, or had time and distance eroded the love they once felt for each other? These questions had plagued her mind ever since she received the letter, but deep down, she knew that God was in control. If it was His will, their love would be renewed, stronger than ever before.

Grace dressed quickly, choosing a simple, yet elegant dress that flowed gently around her legs. She glanced at herself in the mirror, smoothing a strand of hair behind her ear. There was a nervous energy in her movements, but also a quiet determination. She was ready to face whatever the day would bring, trusting that God's plan was unfolding exactly as it should.

As she made her way downstairs, the smell of freshly brewed coffee greeted her, filling the air with its rich aroma. She poured herself a cup and stepped out onto the porch, letting the warmth of the sun and the coolness of the breeze wrap around her. This was her sanctuary, the place where she often sat to reflect and find peace.

Grace sipped her coffee slowly, her thoughts drifting back to the last time she had seen Ethan. It had been a bittersweet parting, filled with tears and promises. She remembered the way he had looked at her, his eyes filled with both sadness and hope. He had been torn between his love for her and his desire to pursue his dreams. Grace had understood, even though it had broken her heart to let him go.

She had never told Ethan how deeply she loved him, fearing that it would only make it harder for him to leave. Instead, she had kept her feelings hidden, choosing to support him in his decision and trusting that God would bring them back together when the time was right. But now, with Ethan's return, Grace wondered if she had made the right choice. Should she have fought harder to keep him close, or had she done the right thing by letting him follow his dreams?

The sound of a car pulling up to the curb brought Grace out of her thoughts. She looked up to see a sleek, silver sedan coming to a stop in front of her house. Her heart skipped a beat as the driver's door opened and a tall, familiar figure stepped out. It was Ethan, looking as handsome as ever, with his dark hair slightly tousled and his blue eyes sparkling in the morning light.

Grace's breath caught in her throat as their eyes met. For a moment, time seemed to stand still, and all the years that had passed between them melted away. It was as if nothing had changed, as if they were still the same two kids who had grown up together, sharing dreams and making promises.

Ethan smiled, a smile that reached his eyes and filled them with warmth. "Grace," he said, his voice soft and filled with emotion. "It's so good to see you."

Grace set her coffee cup down on the porch railing and walked toward him, her heart pounding in her chest. "Ethan," she whispered, her voice trembling with emotion. "You're really here."

Ethan closed the distance between them, and before Grace could say another word, he pulled her into a tight embrace. She felt his arms wrap around her, holding her close, and for a moment, she let herself sink into the comfort of his embrace. It was as if all the years of separation had never existed, as if they had always been together.

When they finally pulled apart, Ethan took a step back and looked at her, his gaze filled with tenderness. "I've missed you, Grace. More than you could ever know."

Grace smiled, her eyes filling with tears. "I've missed you too, Ethan. Every single day."

They stood there for a moment, simply looking at each other, letting the reality of the moment sink in. It was a moment that Grace had dreamed of for so long, and now that it was here, she felt a sense of peace that she hadn't felt in years.

"Come inside," she said, finally breaking the silence. "We have so much to catch up on."

Ethan nodded, and together they walked into the house, the place that had been a second home to him for so many years. As they entered the living room, memories flooded back, memories of the countless hours they had spent here, talking, laughing, and dreaming about the future.

Grace led him to the couch, and they sat down, facing each other. For a moment, neither of them spoke, each lost in their own thoughts. Then, finally, Ethan broke the silence.

"Grace," he began, his voice filled with a seriousness that caught her attention. "There's something I need to tell you, something I've been carrying with me for a long time."

Grace's heart skipped a beat as she looked at him, her mind racing with possibilities. "What is it, Ethan?" she asked, her voice barely above a whisper.

Ethan took a deep breath, as if gathering the courage to say what was on his mind. "I left Pinebrook all those years ago because I felt that I had to, that I needed to pursue my dreams and make something of myself. But every day that I was away, I couldn't stop thinking about you. No matter where I went or what I did, you were always in my heart."

Grace felt her breath catch in her throat as she listened to his words, her emotions swirling inside her. "Ethan..."

He held up a hand, stopping her from speaking. "Let me finish, Grace. Please."

She nodded, her eyes locked on his.

"I realized something while I was away," Ethan continued, his voice filled with emotion. "I realized that I made a mistake by leaving you. I thought that I could chase my dreams and then come back to you

when I was ready, but what I didn't understand was that you were always my dream. You were the one thing I wanted more than anything else, and I left you behind."

Tears filled Grace's eyes as she listened to Ethan's confession. It was everything she had ever wanted to hear, and yet, it was so much more.

Ethan reached out and took her hands in his, his touch warm and reassuring. "I'm back now, Grace, and I don't want to waste any more time. I know that I made a promise to you all those years ago, and I intend to keep it. I love you, Grace. I always have, and I always will."

Grace felt a sob rise in her throat as she looked at Ethan, the man she had loved for so long. She had dreamed of this moment, of hearing him say those words, and now that it was happening, she felt overwhelmed with emotion.

"Ethan," she whispered, her voice trembling. "I love you too. I always have. I never stopped."

Ethan's eyes filled with tears as he heard her words, and he pulled her into his arms once more, holding her close as they both cried tears of joy and relief. It was a moment that they had both waited for, a moment that marked the beginning of a new chapter in their lives.

As they sat there, wrapped in each other's arms, Grace felt a deep sense of peace settle over her. She knew that this was the beginning of something beautiful, something that had been ordained by God. It was a love that had been promised, a love that had been tested and refined, and now, it was ready to bloom.

In that moment, Grace knew that the promise they had made to each other all those years ago was not just a promise between two people, but a promise from God. It was a promise of love, a love that was grounded in faith, hope, and the belief that true love was a gift from God.

As they pulled apart, Ethan looked into Grace's eyes, his expression filled with determination. "Grace, I want to spend the rest of my life with you. I want to build a future together, one that is grounded in our love for each other and our faith in God. Will you marry me?"

Grace's heart swelled with emotion as she heard his words, and she felt tears fill her eyes once more. "Yes, Ethan," she whispered, her voice filled with love. "Yes, I will marry you."

Ethan's face broke into a wide smile, and he leaned in to kiss her, a kiss that was filled with all the love and passion that they had both held back for so long. It was a kiss that sealed their promise, a promise of love that would last a lifetime.

As they sat together, holding each other close, Grace felt a sense of joy and fulfillment that she had never known before. She knew that their love was a gift from God, a love that had been promised and was now being fulfilled.

In that moment, Grace silently prayed, thanking God for bringing Ethan back into her life and for the love that they shared. She knew that their journey was just beginning, and that there would be challenges ahead, but she also knew that their love was strong enough to overcome anything.

As she finished her prayer, the words of 1 Corinthians 13:13 echoed in her mind once more: "And now these three remain: faith, hope and love. But the greatest of these is love." It was a reminder that love was the greatest gift of all, a gift that came from God and was meant to be cherished and nurtured.

Grace looked at Ethan, her heart filled with love and gratitude. "I love you, Ethan," she said softly. "And I thank God for bringing us together."

Ethan smiled and kissed her forehead. "I love you too, Grace. And I promise to spend the rest of my life showing you just how much."

As they sat together, holding each other close, Grace knew that their love was a promise that would never be broken. It was a promise grounded in faith, hope, and the belief that true love was a gift from God, a love that would last forever.

Theological Reflection

AS WE REFLECT ON THE promise of love, we are reminded of the words of the Apostle Paul in 1 Corinthians 13:13: "And now these three remain: faith, hope and love. But the greatest of these is love." Love, as described in the Bible, is more than just a feeling or emotion. It is a commitment, a covenant, and a reflection of God's love for us.

In the story of Grace and Ethan, we see how love is tested, refined, and ultimately fulfilled. Their journey reminds us that true love is not always easy, and it often requires sacrifice, patience, and faith. But when love is grounded in God, it becomes a powerful force that can overcome any obstacle.

The promise of love is not just a promise between two people, but a promise from God. It is a promise that He will be with us, guiding us and strengthening us as we navigate the challenges of life. When we place our trust in God and allow His love to fill our hearts, we can experience the fullness of love as He intended.

As we journey through life, may we always remember that love is the greatest gift of all. It is a gift that comes from God, and it is meant to be shared, nurtured, and cherished. When we make a promise of love, let it be a reflection of the love that God has for us, a love that is eternal and unchanging.

May we always strive to love others as God loves us, with a love that is patient, kind, and enduring. And may we always hold fast to the promise of love, knowing that it is a gift from God, a gift that will never fade away.

Chapter 2: Faith in Love

The day dawned with a promise of warmth, but there was a lingering chill in the air that matched the unease Grace Elliott felt deep within her heart. The sun, which had been so bright and welcoming the day before, was now shrouded by clouds that rolled across the sky in a slow, ominous dance. It was as if the world itself sensed the uncertainty that had settled between her and Ethan Matthews, the man she loved more than life itself.

It had been just a week since Ethan's return to Pinebrook, a week filled with joy, laughter, and the rekindling of a love that had never truly faded. But with the joy had come the inevitable challenges, challenges that threatened to shake the very foundation of the promise they had made to each other. Grace had always known that love required more than just feelings; it required faith—faith in each other and faith in God's plan. Yet, knowing this did little to ease the worry that gnawed at her heart.

Grace stood by the kitchen window, her hands wrapped around a warm cup of tea, her gaze fixed on the gray horizon. The sound of the kettle whistling softly in the background was a comforting noise, grounding her in the familiar routine of the morning. But even as she sipped the soothing liquid, her thoughts were miles away, tangled in the complexities of the situation that had arisen between her and Ethan.

Ethan had been called back to the city for a medical emergency at the hospital where he worked. It was the kind of situation that had always pulled him away, the kind of responsibility that had led him to leave Pinebrook in the first place. Grace understood the importance of his work—he was a brilliant doctor, dedicated to saving lives—but understanding didn't make the sudden departure any easier to bear.

They had barely begun to rediscover each other when the call had come, interrupting their newfound peace. Ethan's face had gone pale when he answered the phone, his eyes reflecting the gravity of the situation. "Grace, I'm so sorry," he had said, his voice filled with regret. "I have to go. It's an emergency."

Grace had forced a smile, pushing down the disappointment that threatened to spill over. "I understand, Ethan. You have to do what you have to do."

He had taken her hand then, squeezing it tightly as if trying to convey all the things he couldn't say. "I'll be back as soon as I can. I promise."

She had nodded, but the words had felt hollow, as if they couldn't quite bridge the gap that had suddenly opened between them. Ethan had kissed her goodbye, his lips lingering on hers as if reluctant to leave, and then he was gone, the sound of his car fading into the distance.

Now, days later, Grace found herself questioning everything. Had they been foolish to think they could simply pick up where they left off? Could their love survive the demands of Ethan's career and the distance that would inevitably come between them? And more importantly, could she have faith in their love, in the promise they had made to each other, even when it seemed that life was conspiring to keep them apart?

The questions swirled in her mind like the dark clouds overhead, and Grace felt a tear slip down her cheek. She had prayed for strength, for faith to trust in God's plan, but the uncertainty was overwhelming. What if this was just the beginning of a series of challenges that would test their love to its limits? What if they weren't strong enough to endure?

A soft knock at the front door pulled Grace from her thoughts. She wiped her eyes quickly and set down her cup, hurrying to answer the door. When she opened it, she was surprised to find her best friend, Rachel, standing on the porch, a concerned look on her face.

"Grace," Rachel said, her voice gentle as she stepped inside and pulled Grace into a hug. "I had a feeling you might need someone to talk to."

Grace returned the hug, feeling a rush of gratitude for her friend's intuition. Rachel had always been there for her, through the highs and lows of life, and today was no different.

"I'm so glad you're here," Grace admitted as they moved to the living room. "I've been feeling so lost."

Rachel sat down beside her on the couch, her expression filled with empathy. "It's Ethan, isn't it?"

Grace nodded, feeling the tears welling up again. "He had to leave so suddenly, and I know it's because of his job, but... I just don't know if I can do this. I don't know if I have the strength to keep believing that everything will work out."

Rachel took her hand, squeezing it gently. "Grace, love isn't easy. It never is. But you've always been one of the strongest people I know, and your faith has always been your anchor. You've taught me so much about trusting in God's plan, even when things don't make sense."

Grace let out a shaky breath. "I'm trying, Rachel. I really am. But it feels like this is just the first of many challenges, and I'm scared. I'm scared that we won't be able to hold on."

Rachel nodded, understanding the weight of Grace's fears. "It's okay to be scared, Grace. But remember, faith isn't about having all the answers. It's about trusting that God does. Hebrews 11:1 says, 'Now faith is the substance of things hoped for, the evidence of things not seen.' You may not see how everything will work out right now, but that's where faith comes in."

Grace knew Rachel was right, but it didn't make the fear go away. She had always believed in God's plan, had always trusted that He would guide her steps, but this felt different. This felt like a test she wasn't sure she could pass.

"What if I'm not strong enough?" Grace whispered, voicing her deepest fear.

Rachel's expression softened, and she reached out to cup Grace's face in her hands. "Grace, you don't have to be strong enough on your own. God's strength is made perfect in our weakness. You're not alone in this. You have Ethan, you have me, and most importantly, you have God. And He will carry you through this, just as He always has."

Grace closed her eyes, letting Rachel's words wash over her. She knew her friend was right. She knew that God had always been there for her, guiding her through the darkest moments of her life. But knowing and believing were two different things, and in this moment, she needed to believe.

When Grace opened her eyes again, there was a new resolve in them. "You're right, Rachel. I need to trust in God's plan, even when I don't understand it. I need to have faith in the love that Ethan and I share, and believe that it's strong enough to withstand whatever comes our way."

Rachel smiled, her eyes filled with pride. "That's the Grace I know. And remember, you don't have to go through this alone. I'm here for you, and so is God."

Grace nodded, feeling a renewed sense of peace settle over her. She knew that the road ahead wouldn't be easy, but she also knew that she didn't have to walk it alone. With God by her side, she could face whatever challenges came her way, and with Ethan's love, she could weather any storm.

As Rachel left, Grace returned to the kitchen, her heart lighter than it had been all morning. She picked up her Bible from the counter, flipping through the pages until she found the verse that Rachel had quoted earlier: Hebrews 11:1. She read the words aloud, letting them sink into her soul.

"Now faith is the substance of things hoped for, the evidence of things not seen."

Grace knew that faith wasn't about having all the answers or knowing exactly how things would turn out. It was about trusting in God's plan, even when the path was unclear. It was about believing that the love she and Ethan shared was strong enough to overcome any obstacle, even when the future seemed uncertain.

She closed the Bible and bowed her head in prayer, asking God for the strength to hold on to that faith, to trust in His plan, and to believe in the promise of love that He had placed in her heart.

The days that followed Ethan's departure were long and filled with uncertainty. Grace went about her daily routine, trying to keep busy and not dwell on the thoughts that threatened to overwhelm her. But no matter how much she tried to distract herself, the worry remained, lurking just beneath the surface.

Ethan had called a few times, each conversation brief and filled with updates on the situation at the hospital. He was exhausted, that much was clear, and the weight of his responsibilities was evident in his voice. But despite the distance and the challenges he was facing, Ethan always made sure to reassure

Grace that he was thinking of her, that he missed her, and that he would be back as soon as he could.

"I hate that I had to leave so suddenly," Ethan had said during one of their calls, his voice filled with regret. "But I promise you, Grace, I'll make it up to you. I'll be back soon."

Grace had forced a smile, even though he couldn't see it. "I know you will, Ethan. Just take care of yourself, okay?"

"I will," he had replied, his tone softening. "I love you, Grace."

"I love you too," she had whispered, holding back the tears that threatened to fall.

But as the days turned into a week, and then another, Grace began to feel the strain of the distance. She knew that Ethan's work was important, that he was saving lives and making a difference, but

it didn't make the loneliness any easier to bear. She missed him more than she could put into words, missed the sound of his voice, the touch of his hand, the way he made her feel safe and loved.

One evening, after another long day, Grace found herself sitting on the porch, staring out at the fading light of the sunset. The sky was painted in shades of orange and pink, the colors blending together in a beautiful display of God's creation. But even the beauty of the sunset couldn't chase away the emptiness she felt inside.

She pulled her knees up to her chest, wrapping her arms around them as she rested her chin on her knees. The weight of her worries pressed down on her, and for the first time in days, Grace let the tears fall. She cried for the uncertainty of the future, for the fear that their love might not be strong enough to withstand the challenges they were facing, for the loneliness that had taken root in her heart.

As she wept, the words of Hebrews 11:1 echoed in her mind: "Now faith is the substance of things hoped for, the evidence of things not seen." She had been holding on to those words, clinging to them like a lifeline, but in this moment, they felt distant, like a promise that was just out of reach.

"God," Grace whispered through her tears, "I'm trying to have faith, but it's so hard. I feel so lost, so alone. Please, help me to trust in Your plan. Help me to believe that everything will work out, even when I can't see how."

She didn't know how long she sat there, pouring out her heart to God, but eventually, the tears slowed, and a sense of peace began to settle over her. It was a peace that she couldn't explain, a peace that didn't make sense in the midst of her pain, but it was there, wrapping around her like a warm embrace.

Grace took a deep breath, lifting her eyes to the sky. The colors of the sunset had deepened, the vibrant hues now fading into the darkness of night. And yet, as she watched the stars begin to twinkle in the sky, she felt a glimmer of hope take root in her heart.

It wasn't a hope born of certainty or understanding, but a hope born of faith—faith that God was in control, that He had a plan, and that His love would guide her through the darkness. It was the kind of faith that Hebrews 11:1 spoke of, the substance of things hoped for, the evidence of things not seen.

Grace wiped away the last of her tears, feeling a renewed sense of determination. She didn't have all the answers, and she didn't know what the future held, but she knew that she could trust God. She could trust that His love would sustain her, that His plan was perfect, and that He would bring her and Ethan through this trial stronger than before.

With a final look at the stars, Grace stood and made her way back inside. She knew that the days ahead would still be challenging, that there would be moments of doubt and fear, but she also knew that she wasn't alone. God was with her, guiding her every step of the way, and with Him, she could face whatever came.

As the second week of Ethan's absence drew to a close, Grace received a phone call that changed everything. She was in the middle of preparing dinner when her phone rang, the sound startling her from her thoughts. She quickly wiped her hands on a towel and picked up the phone, her heart skipping a beat when she saw Ethan's name on the screen.

"Ethan?" she answered, her voice filled with both hope and apprehension.

"Grace," Ethan's voice came through the line, sounding more tired than she had ever heard it. "I... I don't know how to tell you this, but... I might have to stay here longer than I thought."

Grace felt her heart sink, the hope she had been holding on to slipping through her fingers. "What do you mean? Is everything okay?"

Ethan let out a heavy sigh, and she could hear the exhaustion in his voice. "There's been a complication with one of the patients. It's... it's serious, Grace. I don't think I can leave until we know more."

Grace closed her eyes, feeling the weight of his words settle over her like a lead blanket. "I understand, Ethan. I really do. But... it's just so hard being here without you."

"I know," Ethan said, his voice filled with regret. "And I'm so sorry, Grace. I hate that I'm putting you through this. But I can't just leave these people. They need me."

Grace took a deep breath, trying to keep her voice steady. "I know they do, and I'm proud of you for the work you're doing. But... I need you too, Ethan."

There was a long silence on the other end of the line, and for a moment, Grace feared that she had said too much. But then Ethan spoke, his voice filled with emotion.

"Grace, I love you more than anything in this world. And I promise you, as soon as I can, I'll be back. I just... I need you to have faith in me, in us. Can you do that?"

Grace felt the tears well up in her eyes again, but this time, they were tears of love, of hope, of a faith that was beginning to take root once more. "I do have faith, Ethan. I have faith in you, in us, and in God's plan for our lives. I know that we'll get through this, no matter how long it takes."

Ethan let out a breath that sounded like relief. "Thank you, Grace. That means everything to me. I'll call you as soon as I know more, okay?"

"Okay," Grace whispered, her voice filled with love. "I love you, Ethan. And I'm here, waiting for you, no matter how long it takes."

"I love you too, Grace," Ethan replied, his voice filled with warmth. "And I promise, I'll be back as soon as I can."

When they hung up, Grace stood in the kitchen, the phone still clutched in her hand. The uncertainty was still there, the challenges still loomed ahead, but in that moment, she felt a peace that she hadn't felt in weeks. It was a peace born of faith, a faith that was growing stronger with each passing day.

She knew that their love would be tested, that there would be more challenges to come, but she also knew that they would face them together. And with God's help, their love would not only survive but thrive, becoming stronger and more resilient with each trial they faced.

Grace set the phone down and returned to preparing dinner, a small smile playing on her lips. She knew that the road ahead would be long, but she also knew that she wasn't walking it alone. With Ethan by her side and God guiding their steps, she had faith that they would make it through, stronger and more in love than ever before.

Theological Reflection

FAITH AND LOVE ARE deeply intertwined, each one feeding and sustaining the other in ways that are both powerful and mysterious. Hebrews 11:1 tells us, "Now faith is the substance of things hoped for, the evidence of things not seen." This verse reminds us that faith is not about having all the answers or seeing the full picture. It's about trusting in what we cannot see, believing in the promises of God even when the path is unclear.

In Grace and Ethan's journey, we see how their faith is tested, how the challenges they face threaten to shake the foundation of their love. But it is in these moments of uncertainty and doubt that their faith is most needed. It is their faith in each other, and in God's plan, that carries them through the trials they face.

Love, when grounded in faith, becomes something far greater than a fleeting emotion. It becomes a commitment, a promise that endures through the storms of life. It is a reflection of God's love for us, a love that is steadfast and unchanging, even when we cannot see the way forward.

As we navigate our own lives, we are often faced with situations that challenge our faith, that make us question whether we can truly trust in God's plan. But it is in these moments that we must hold on to the truth of Hebrews 11:1. We may not see the outcome, we may not understand the reasons behind the challenges we face, but we can trust that God is with us, guiding us, and working all things for our good.

When we place our faith in God, we are placing our trust in a love that is perfect, a love that never fails. And when our love for others is rooted in that faith, it becomes a love that can withstand any trial, a love that is strong enough to carry us through the darkest of times.

May we always remember that faith is the substance of things hoped for, the evidence of things not seen. And may our love, grounded in that faith, be a reflection of the divine love that God has for each of us, a love that is eternal and unchanging.

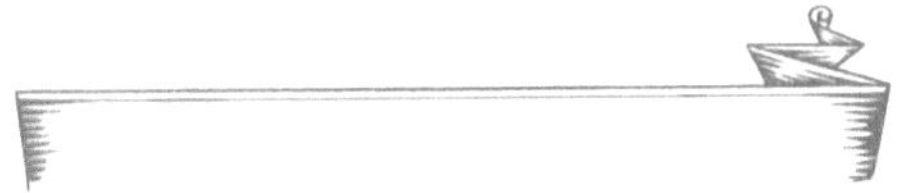

Chapter 3: Sacrificial Love

The air was thick with anticipation as Grace Elliott made her way down the familiar streets of Pinebrook. The early morning sun had barely risen, casting long shadows that danced along the pavement. Despite the beauty of the dawn, there was a heaviness in Grace's heart that she couldn't shake, a weight that had been growing ever since Ethan Matthews had returned to the city weeks ago. Today, however, was different. Today, Grace was determined to make a decision that would change the course of their lives forever.

Grace had always known that love required sacrifice. She had seen it in the lives of her parents, who had given up so much for each other and for their family. She had witnessed it in the small acts of kindness and selflessness that defined the lives of the people in her community. But now, for the first time, Grace found herself standing on the precipice of making a sacrifice that would test the very core of her love for Ethan.

As she walked, her mind replayed the conversation she had with Ethan the night before. He had called, his voice tired and strained, but filled with a quiet determination that Grace knew all too well.

"Grace, I have something important to tell you," Ethan had said, his tone serious.

Grace had braced herself, sensing that whatever he was about to say would be significant. "What is it, Ethan?"

There had been a long pause, as if Ethan was gathering the strength to speak. "I've been offered a permanent position here at the hospital," he finally said, his words heavy with meaning. "It's an incredible opportunity, Grace. A chance to do the kind of work I've always dreamed of. But... it means I won't be coming back to Pinebrook."

The words had hit Grace like a punch to the gut, stealing the breath from her lungs. She had known that this was a possibility, that Ethan's career might take him away from Pinebrook, but hearing it confirmed had made the fear she had been carrying for so long a reality.

Grace had struggled to find her voice, the pain in her chest almost unbearable. "But Ethan... what about us?"

Ethan had let out a deep sigh, the weariness in his voice palpable. "That's why I'm calling, Grace. I don't want to lose you. I love you, and I want us to be together. But I also know that asking you to leave Pinebrook, to leave everything you've ever known, is a huge sacrifice."

Grace had felt the tears well up in her eyes, her heart breaking at the thought of leaving Pinebrook, the town that had been her home for her entire life. She had grown up here, surrounded by the love of her family and friends, and the thought of leaving it all behind was almost too much to bear. But as she had listened to Ethan's voice, filled with both hope and fear, she had realized that she was faced with a choice—a choice that would define their future.

"I need time to think, Ethan," Grace had finally said, her voice trembling with emotion. "This is... this is a lot to take in."

Ethan had understood, his voice soft and filled with love. "I know, Grace. Take all the time you need. Just know that whatever you decide, I'll support you. I just want you to be happy."

As Grace had hung up the phone, the tears had fallen freely, the weight of the decision pressing down on her like a thousand pounds. She had spent the night praying, asking God for guidance, for the strength to make the right choice. And as the dawn had broken, a sense of clarity had begun to settle over her.

Now, as she approached the small church that had been her sanctuary for so many years, Grace knew that the time had come to make her decision. She pushed open the heavy wooden door, the familiar scent of incense and old wood filling her senses as she stepped inside. The church was empty, the morning light streaming through the stained glass windows, casting colorful patterns on the stone floor.

Grace made her way to the front pew and knelt down, her hands clasped together in prayer. The silence of the church was comforting, a reminder that she was not alone in this. She closed her eyes and took a deep breath, letting the stillness wash over her.

"Lord," she whispered, her voice trembling with emotion, "I don't know what to do. I love Ethan with all my heart, but the thought of leaving Pinebrook... it terrifies me. This is my home, my family, my life. But I know that love requires sacrifice, and I'm willing to do whatever it takes to be with him. Please, Lord, show me the way. Help me to make the right decision."

As she prayed, the words of John 15:13 came to her mind: "Greater love has no one than this: to lay down one's life for one's friends." Grace had always known that love was about more than just feelings. It was about putting the needs of others before her own, about being willing to make sacrifices for the people she loved. And now, she realized, she was being called to make the greatest sacrifice of all.

Grace opened her eyes and looked up at the altar, the crucifix that hung above it a reminder of the ultimate sacrifice that had been made for her. Jesus had laid down His life for her, for all of humanity, out of love. And now, she was being called to lay down her life in a different way, to give up the life she had known for the love she had found with Ethan.

It was a daunting thought, one that filled her with both fear and hope. But as she knelt there in the quiet of the church, Grace felt a sense of peace begin to settle over her. She knew what she had to do. She had to trust in God's plan, to have faith that this was the path she was meant to take. And with that faith, she knew that she could make the sacrifice that love required.

Grace rose to her feet, her heart still heavy but filled with a newfound determination. She knew that the road ahead would not be easy, that there would be moments of doubt and fear. But she also knew that she was not alone. God was with her, guiding her steps, and with His help, she could make the sacrifice that love demanded.

As she left the church and made her way back home, Grace felt a sense of clarity that she hadn't felt in weeks. She knew that her decision would change everything, but she also knew that it was the right one. She loved Ethan, and she was willing to make the sacrifice to be with him. Because that was what love was about—putting the needs of the person you loved above your own, even when it meant giving up something precious.

The walk back home was filled with a mix of emotions—fear, sadness, hope, and love. Grace knew that she was leaving behind a life that had been filled with so much joy, but she also knew that she was stepping into a future filled with the promise of a love that had been tested and proven strong.

When Grace arrived home, she found Rachel waiting for her on the porch, her expression filled with concern. "Grace, where have you been? I've been worried about you."

Grace offered her friend a small smile as she sat down beside her. "I needed to pray, to think about everything that's been happening."

Rachel reached out and took Grace's hand, squeezing it gently. "And have you come to a decision?"

Grace nodded, her heart pounding in her chest. "Yes, I have. I'm going to move to the city with Ethan."

Rachel's eyes widened in surprise, but there was no judgment in her gaze, only understanding. "That's a big decision, Grace. Are you sure it's what you want?"

Grace took a deep breath, her gaze steady. "I'm sure, Rachel. I love Pinebrook, and it will always be my home. But I love Ethan more, and I believe that God has a plan for us. I'm willing to make this sacrifice because I know that our love is worth it."

Rachel nodded, a proud smile on her lips. "I'm so proud of you, Grace. You're one of the strongest people I know, and I have no doubt that you'll thrive wherever you go."

Grace felt a tear slip down her cheek as she squeezed Rachel's hand. "Thank you, Rachel. I couldn't have made this decision without your support."

Rachel pulled Grace into a hug, holding her close. "You're going to be okay, Grace. And I'll always be here for you, no matter where you are."

As they sat there, wrapped in each other's embrace, Grace felt a sense of peace wash over her. She knew that the road ahead would be filled with challenges, but she also knew that she was not alone. She had Ethan, she had Rachel, and most importantly, she had God. And with their love and support, she knew that she could face whatever came her way.

The days that followed were filled with preparations for Grace's move to the city. There were goodbyes to be said, belongings to be packed, and a future to be planned. But through it all, Grace felt a sense of calm that she hadn't expected.

She knew that she was making the right decision, and that knowledge gave her the strength to face the inevitable challenges that lay ahead.

Ethan had been overjoyed when Grace had told him of her decision. He had immediately started making plans for their new life together, and the excitement in his voice had been contagious. Grace had felt her own excitement grow as they talked about their future, about the home they would make together and the life they would build.

But as the day of her departure approached, Grace found herself grappling with a mix of emotions. There was the excitement of starting a new life with the man she loved, but there was also the sadness of leaving behind everything she had ever known. Pinebrook had been her home for so long, and the thought of leaving it behind was bittersweet.

The night before her departure, Grace found herself walking through the town, taking in the sights and sounds that had been a part of her life for so many years. She walked past the old bookstore where she had spent countless hours lost in the pages of her favorite novels. She passed the park where she had played as a child, the swings still creaking softly in the evening breeze. She walked by the church, the place where she had found solace and strength in her darkest moments.

As she walked, memories flooded her mind—memories of a life filled with love, laughter, and community. It was a life that she would always cherish, a life that had shaped her into the person she was today. But it was also a life that she was willing to leave behind for the love she had found with Ethan.

When Grace finally returned home, she found her parents waiting for her on the porch, their faces filled with a mixture of pride and sadness. They had always known that this day would come, that Grace would one day spread her wings and fly. But knowing didn't make the goodbye any easier.

Grace walked up the steps and wrapped her arms around her parents, holding them close. "I'm going to miss you both so much," she whispered, her voice thick with emotion.

Her mother stroked her hair, her own voice trembling. "We're going to miss you too, sweetheart. But we're so proud of you. You've grown into an amazing woman, and we know that you're going to do great things."

Her father placed a gentle kiss on her forehead, his eyes shining with tears. "We love you, Grace. And we'll always be here for you, no matter where you are."

Grace nodded, her heart swelling with love for her parents. "I love you both so much."

They stood there for a long moment, wrapped in each other's embrace, the weight of the goodbye pressing down on them. But there was also a sense of peace, a knowing that this was the next step in Grace's journey, a journey that was guided by love and faith.

The next morning, as the sun began to rise, Grace stood by the front door, her bags packed and ready to go. Ethan's car was parked in the driveway, the engine idling softly as he waited for her. Grace took one last look around the house, the place where she had grown up, the place that had been filled with so much love.

Her parents stood beside her, their eyes filled with pride and love. "Are you ready, sweetheart?" her mother asked, her voice gentle.

Grace nodded, a small smile on her lips. "Yes, I'm ready."

With one last hug and a promise to visit soon, Grace stepped out the door and made her way to the car. Ethan was waiting for her, his face lighting up as she approached. "Are you sure about this?" he asked, his voice filled with both excitement and concern.

Grace looked at him, her heart swelling with love. "I've never been more sure about anything in my life, Ethan. I love you, and I'm ready to start our life together."

Ethan's face broke into a wide smile as he pulled her into his arms. "I love you too, Grace. And I promise, I'll make this worth the sacrifice."

Grace knew that he would. She knew that their love was worth everything she was giving up, that the sacrifice she was making was a reflection of the depth of her love for him. It was a love that was grounded in faith, a love that was willing to lay down everything for the sake of the other.

As they drove away from Pinebrook, Grace felt a mix of emotions—sadness, excitement, fear, and hope. But above all, she felt a sense of peace. She knew that she was walking the path that God had set before her, a path that was guided by love and faith.

The road ahead was uncertain, but Grace knew that she wasn't walking it alone. With Ethan by her side and God guiding their steps, she knew that they could face whatever challenges came their way. And with the sacrificial love they shared, she knew that their bond would only grow stronger with time.

Theological Reflection

SACRIFICIAL LOVE IS at the heart of the Christian faith. It is the kind of love that Jesus demonstrated when He laid down His life for us, a love that is selfless, unconditional, and willing to give everything for the sake of others. In John 15:13, Jesus says, "Greater love has no one than this: to lay down one's life for one's friends." This verse speaks to the depth of love that God calls us to, a love that goes beyond mere feelings and actions, and into the realm of true sacrifice.

In Grace's journey, we see a reflection of this sacrificial love. Her decision to leave behind the life she has known, to give up everything for the love she shares with Ethan, is a testament to the depth of her love. It is a love that is willing to make the ultimate sacrifice, to lay down her own desires and needs for the sake of the person she loves.

This kind of love is not easy. It requires strength, courage, and a deep trust in God's plan. It is a love that is willing to walk through the fire, to face challenges and difficulties, all for the sake of the other. But it is also a love that brings with it a deep sense of peace and fulfillment, a knowing that the sacrifice is worth it, because it is grounded in a love that is true and pure.

As we reflect on the sacrificial nature of love, we are reminded of the example that Jesus set for us. He laid down His life for us, not because we deserved it, but because He loved us with an everlasting love. He showed us what it means to love selflessly, to put the needs of others above our own, and to trust in God's plan, even when it requires sacrifice.

May we strive to love others with this kind of sacrificial love, a love that reflects the heart of God. And may we find the strength and courage to make the sacrifices that love requires, knowing that in doing so, we are walking in the footsteps of Jesus, who showed us the greatest love of all.

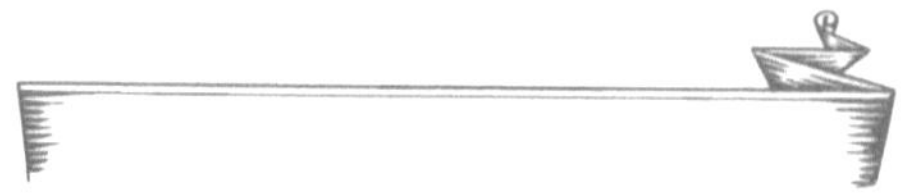

Chapter 4: Love in Trials

The storm clouds rolled in swiftly, dark and menacing, blotting out the sun that had shone so brightly just hours before. The wind howled through the trees, bending their branches under its fierce command, and the first drops of rain began to fall, heavy and cold, as if the heavens themselves were mourning. The storm was not just outside, but also inside the hearts of Grace Elliott and Ethan Matthews. Their love, which had seemed so strong and unshakable, was now being tested in ways they had never imagined.

It had been three months since Grace had made the difficult decision to leave her hometown of Pinebrook and move to the city to be with Ethan. The transition had been challenging, filled with moments of doubt and homesickness, but their love had carried them through. They had built a life together, full of hope and dreams for the future, but now, that life was being threatened by a trial so severe that it threatened to tear them apart.

Ethan paced the length of their small apartment, his face a mask of frustration and worry. He had always been the one who kept his composure, who found solutions to problems and navigated through challenges with calm determination. But now, he felt as if the ground beneath him was shifting, leaving him unsteady and unsure.

Grace sat on the edge of the couch, her hands clasped tightly in her lap, her heart aching with the weight of their situation. She had never seen Ethan like this, and it frightened her. The man she loved, who had always been her rock, was struggling, and she didn't know how to help him.

"Ethan," she began softly, her voice trembling with emotion. "Please, talk to me. We can't get through this if we don't face it together."

Ethan stopped pacing and turned to look at her, his eyes filled with a mixture of pain and helplessness. "Grace, I don't know what to do. I've always been able to fix things, to find a way through, but this... this is different."

Grace's heart broke at the sight of his despair. She rose from the couch and crossed the room to stand before him, reaching out to take his hands in hers. "We've always faced everything together, Ethan. We've always been able to rely on each other and on our faith. This time is no different. We can get through this, but we have to do it together."

Ethan closed his eyes, taking a deep breath as he tried to steady himself. He knew she was right, but the fear that had taken root in his heart was hard to shake. He opened his eyes and looked at her, his expression softening as he saw the love and determination in her gaze.

"I'm scared, Grace," he admitted, his voice barely above a whisper. "I'm scared that I'm going to lose everything—my job, our home, and... and you."

Grace felt tears prick at the corners of her eyes as she listened to his confession. She had always known that Ethan was carrying the weight of the world on his shoulders, but hearing him voice his fears made her realize just how much he had been struggling.

"You're not going to lose me," she said firmly, squeezing his hands. "No matter what happens, I'm here, and I'm not going anywhere. We'll face this trial together, and we'll come out stronger on the other side. But we have to trust in each other and in God's plan."

Ethan looked at her, his heart swelling with love and gratitude. He didn't know how he had been blessed with such an incredible woman, but he thanked God every day for bringing her into his life. She was his strength, his anchor, and he knew that he couldn't face this trial without her.

"I don't deserve you," he whispered, pulling her into his arms and holding her close.

Grace buried her face in his chest, her tears finally spilling over as she clung to him. "We deserve each other," she replied softly. "And we deserve to be happy, no matter what life throws at us."

They stood there for a long moment, wrapped in each other's embrace, finding comfort in the closeness of their love. The storm outside raged on, but inside, they found a small measure of peace in knowing that they would face whatever came together.

The trial they faced had begun a few weeks earlier when Ethan's job at the hospital had come under threat. The hospital was facing severe budget cuts, and rumors had been circulating that layoffs were imminent. Ethan, who had always been dedicated to his work, found himself caught in the crossfire of administrative decisions that were beyond his control.

He had been called into his supervisor's office one afternoon and told that his position was being eliminated as part of the hospital's restructuring efforts. The news had hit him like a ton of bricks, leaving him reeling with shock and disbelief. For years, he had poured his heart and soul into his work, and now, it was being taken away from him in the blink of an eye.

Ethan had returned home that evening, his face pale and his eyes hollow, as he broke the news to Grace. She had listened in stunned silence as he explained the situation, her heart breaking for him as she saw the pain etched in his expression. He had always been so proud of his work, and now, it was being stripped away from him.

Grace had tried to be strong, to offer words of comfort and reassurance, but inside, she was filled with fear. She knew how much his job meant to him, how much of his identity was tied to his work as a doctor. And now, without it, she worried about what would happen to him, to them.

The days that followed were filled with uncertainty and anxiety. Ethan spent hours on the phone with colleagues, trying to find a way to save his job, but every effort seemed to be met with dead ends. The hospital was adamant in its decision, and there was nothing Ethan could do to change it.

Grace watched as Ethan became more withdrawn, the stress of their situation taking a toll on him. He barely slept, and when he did, it was fitful and restless. He stopped eating, his appetite gone as worry consumed him. And through it all, Grace felt helpless, unable to do anything to ease his pain.

The strain of the trial began to take a toll on their relationship as well. The once easy and natural communication between them became stilted and strained. Ethan, who had always been open with his thoughts and feelings, began to shut down, retreating into himself as he tried to grapple with the loss of his job and the uncertainty of their future.

Grace tried to reach out to him, to offer her support, but her efforts were often met with frustration and anger. Ethan would snap at her, his words sharp and hurtful, and she would retreat, feeling hurt and confused. She knew that he was hurting, that he was lashing out because he didn't know how to deal with the pain, but it didn't make the hurt any less real.

The tension between them grew, and for the first time, Grace began to fear that their love might not survive this trial. She had always believed that their love was strong enough to overcome anything, but now, she wasn't so sure. The fear that they might lose each other began to take root in her heart, and she found herself questioning everything.

It was during one of their many arguments that things finally came to a head. Ethan had come home late, his face drawn and tired, and Grace had confronted him about his behavior. The argument that followed was heated, filled with accusations and hurtful words, and it ended with Ethan storming out of the apartment, slamming the door behind him.

Grace had stood in the middle of the living room, her heart pounding in her chest as the reality of what had just happened sank in. She had never seen Ethan so angry, and the thought that he might not come back terrified her. She sank down onto the couch, her hands shaking as tears filled her eyes.

"God," she whispered, her voice trembling with emotion. "Please, help us. I don't know what to do. I don't want to lose him, but I don't know how to fix this."

She sat there in the silence, the only sound the rain tapping against the windows, as she prayed for guidance, for strength, for the love that she and Ethan shared to endure this trial.

HOURS PASSED, AND THE storm outside began to ease, the wind dying down and the rain tapering off into a gentle drizzle. The apartment was dark, the only light coming from the dim glow of a lamp in the corner. Grace had fallen into a fitful sleep on the couch, her body and mind exhausted from the emotional turmoil of the evening.

She was startled awake by the sound of the door opening, her heart leaping into her throat as she saw Ethan step inside. He looked drenched, his clothes soaked from the rain, but there was a look of determination in his eyes that she hadn't seen in days.

"Grace," he said softly, his voice filled with remorse. "I'm sorry."

Grace sat up, her heart pounding as she looked at him, unsure of what to say.

Ethan closed the door behind him and crossed the room to kneel before her, taking her hands in his. "I'm sorry for everything," he continued, his voice breaking. "I've been so lost in my own pain and fear that I've shut you out. I've hurt you, and I hate myself for it. But I'm here now, and I'm ready to face this with you. If you'll have me."

Grace felt the tears well up in her eyes as she looked at him, her heart swelling with love and relief. "Ethan," she whispered, her voice trembling. "I never wanted anything else. I just wanted you to let me in, to let me help you."

Ethan nodded, his eyes filled with tears as he squeezed her hands. "I know. I've been so scared, Grace. Scared of losing everything, of losing you. But I realize now that I don't have to face this alone. We're stronger together, and I want us to face this trial together, no matter what comes."

Grace let out a sob of relief as she wrapped her arms around him, holding him close. "We will," she whispered. "We'll get through this together."

They sat there for a long time, holding each other as the storm outside finally came to an end. The trial they faced was far from over, but in that moment, they knew that their love was strong enough to endure it. They had found their way back to each other, and with their faith in God and in each other, they knew that they could face whatever challenges lay ahead.

In the days that followed, Grace and Ethan worked to rebuild the bond that had been strained by the trial they were facing. They spent hours talking, sharing their fears and hopes, and finding comfort in each other's presence. It wasn't easy—there were still moments of doubt and worry—but they faced those moments together, leaning on each other and on their faith to carry them through.

Ethan began looking for new job opportunities, determined to find a way to support them and rebuild the life they had begun to create. It was a difficult process, filled with setbacks and disappointments, but Grace was by his side every step of the way, offering her support and encouragement.

Their love, which had been tested by the trial they faced, grew stronger with each passing day. They learned to rely on each other in new ways, to communicate openly and honestly, and to trust that their love was strong enough to endure whatever challenges life threw at them.

One evening, as they sat together on the couch, Grace took Ethan's hand and looked into his eyes. "Ethan," she began softly, "I know this hasn't been easy, but I believe that God has a plan for us. I don't know what the future holds, but I know that as long as we face it together, we can get through anything."

Ethan smiled, squeezing her hand as he nodded. "I believe that too, Grace. This trial has shown me that our love is stronger than I ever imagined. And I'm grateful for that, even though it's been hard."

Grace leaned her head on his shoulder, feeling a sense of peace settle over her. "James 1:2-4 says, 'Consider it pure joy, my brothers and sisters, whenever you face trials of many kinds, because you know that the testing of your faith produces perseverance. Let perseverance finish its work so that you may be mature and complete, not lacking anything.' I think that's what this trial has done for us, Ethan. It's produced perseverance in us, and it's made our love stronger."

Ethan nodded, his heart swelling with love and gratitude for the woman beside him. "You're right, Grace. This trial has been hard, but it's also been a blessing in disguise. It's shown us what we're capable of, and it's deepened our love in ways I never thought possible."

Grace smiled, feeling a sense of hope and joy that she hadn't felt in a long time. "I love you, Ethan," she whispered, her voice filled with emotion. "And I'm so grateful that we've faced this trial together."

Ethan leaned down and kissed her forehead, his heart overflowing with love. "I love you too, Grace. And I'm grateful for you every single day."

As they sat together, holding each other close, they knew that the trial they had faced had brought them closer together, had deepened their love and strengthened their bond. It had been a difficult journey, but it was one that they had faced together, and they had come out the other side stronger and more in love than ever before.

They knew that there would be more trials to come, that life would continue to throw challenges their way, but they also knew that they were ready to face those challenges together. Their love had been tested, and it had endured. And with that knowledge, they faced the future with hope, knowing that whatever came, they would face it together, with their love and faith as their guiding light.

Theological Reflection

TRIALS ARE AN INEVITABLE part of life, and they often come when we least expect them. They can be painful, challenging, and even overwhelming, but they also have the power to shape us, to strengthen our faith, and to deepen our love. In James 1:2-4, we are encouraged to "consider it pure joy" when we face trials, because these trials test our faith and produce perseverance. This perseverance, in turn, helps us to grow, to become mature and complete, not lacking anything.

In Grace and Ethan's journey, we see the truth of this scripture played out in their lives. The trial they faced was a severe one, threatening to break the bond they shared and to take away everything they had worked so hard to build. But through the trial, they learned to rely on each other in new ways, to communicate openly and honestly, and to trust that their love was strong enough to endure whatever challenges came their way.

Their faith was tested, but it was also strengthened. They learned to lean on God and on each other, to find strength in their love and in the knowledge that they were not alone. And through the trial, their love grew deeper, stronger, and more resilient.

This is the power of love in trials—it has the ability to endure, to grow, and to become something even more beautiful than before. It is through the testing of our faith, through the challenges we face, that our love is refined, purified, and made stronger.

As we reflect on the trials we face in our own lives, may we remember the words of James 1:2-4, and consider it pure joy, knowing that these trials are not meant to break us, but to build us up. May we trust in God's plan, knowing that He is with us every step of the way, and that He is using these trials to produce perseverance in us, to make us mature and complete, not lacking anything.

And may we hold fast to the love we share with others, knowing that true love is not just about the good times, but about standing together in the face of trials, trusting that our love will endure, and that it will be stronger on the other side.

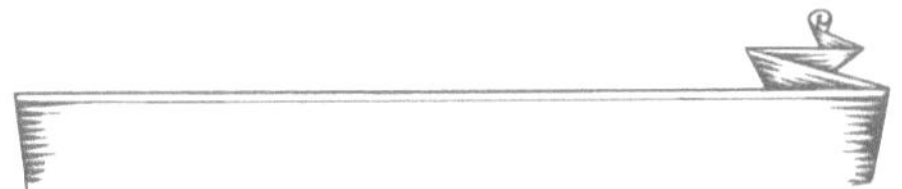

Chapter 5: Forgiveness in Love

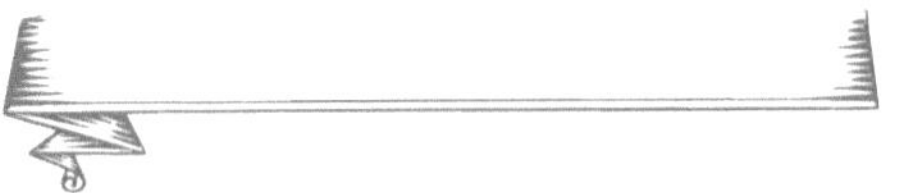

The warmth of the afternoon sun filtered through the sheer curtains of the small, cozy apartment that Grace Elliott and Ethan Matthews called home. It was a quiet day, the kind that usually filled Grace with a sense of contentment as she went about her daily routine. But today was different. Today, the air was thick with tension, the kind of tension that only silence can breed. Grace's heart was heavy as she sat on the edge of the bed, her thoughts swirling in a storm of confusion and hurt.

The source of her pain sat just outside the bedroom door—Ethan, the man she loved more than anything in the world. But love, she was learning, wasn't always enough to protect them from the harsh realities of life. The conflict that had erupted between them the night before had left a chasm that felt impossible to cross. Harsh words had been exchanged, words that had cut deeper than either of them had intended. And now, they found themselves at a crossroads, unsure of how to move forward.

Grace's mind replayed the argument over and over, each time the sting of Ethan's words slicing through her like a knife. They had fought before, of course—what couple didn't? But this time, it felt different. This time, the argument had unearthed something deeper, something more painful, something that wouldn't be so easily mended.

It had all started with something small, as most arguments do. Ethan had been late coming home from work, again. It wasn't unusual for him to get caught up in his duties at the hospital, but Grace had been feeling increasingly isolated and lonely, especially since moving to the city to be with him. She had given up so much—her hometown, her friends, her sense of security—to build a life with Ethan, and while she didn't regret her decision, the transition had been harder than she had anticipated.

The loneliness had been creeping in, slowly at first, but growing stronger with each passing day. She had tried to push it aside, to focus on the love she and Ethan shared, but the more time he spent at work, the more she felt the weight of that loneliness pressing down on her. And when he had walked through the door late, once again, the dam that had been holding back her emotions finally broke.

"Ethan," she had said, trying to keep the frustration out of her voice, "we need to talk."

Ethan had looked at her, tired and worn from the long day, and she had seen the flicker of irritation in his eyes. "Can it wait, Grace? I'm exhausted."

But Grace had reached her breaking point, and she wasn't willing to let it go. "No, it can't wait. We need to talk about what's going on between us."

Ethan had sighed, running a hand through his hair as he sat down on the couch. "What do you mean, 'what's going on between us'? Nothing's going on, Grace. I'm just busy with work."

Grace had felt the anger rising in her chest, the words spilling out before she could stop them. "It's not just work, Ethan. You're never here. You're always at the hospital, and I'm starting to feel like I don't even matter to you anymore."

Ethan had looked at her, his eyes narrowing in frustration. "That's not fair, Grace. You know how important my job is. I'm doing this for us, to build a future for us."

But Grace had shaken her head, the tears welling up in her eyes. "I know your job is important, Ethan, but so is our relationship. And right now, it feels like I'm the only one who cares about making it work."

That was when things had taken a turn. The words that followed had been laced with bitterness and resentment, and before either of them knew it, they were shouting at each other, each trying to make the other understand their pain. But instead of finding common ground, they had only driven each other further apart.

Ethan had said things that Grace knew he didn't mean, but that didn't make them hurt any less. And Grace had retaliated with her own harsh words, words that she now wished she could take back. But the damage had been done, and the rift between them had only widened.

Now, as Grace sat on the bed, she felt the weight of those words pressing down on her, threatening to suffocate her. She loved Ethan, of that she was certain, but she didn't know how to move past the hurt that had been inflicted. How could they go back to the way things were when the trust between them had been so deeply shaken?

A soft knock on the bedroom door pulled Grace from her thoughts. She looked up to see Ethan standing in the doorway, his expression hesitant, almost fearful, as if he wasn't sure if he was welcome.

"Grace," he said softly, his voice tinged with regret, "can we talk?"

Grace felt her heart ache at the sight of him, the man she loved, standing there with so much pain in his eyes. She wanted to run to him, to wrap her arms around him and tell him that everything would be okay. But the hurt was still too fresh, too raw.

"I don't know if I'm ready to talk, Ethan," she admitted, her voice barely above a whisper.

Ethan nodded, stepping into the room and closing the door behind him. He moved slowly, as if unsure of how to approach her, and finally sat down on the edge of the bed, leaving a space between them.

"I understand," he said, his voice filled with sorrow. "I just... I just wanted to say that I'm sorry, Grace. I know I hurt you last night, and I hate myself for it. I didn't mean the things I said. I was just... I don't know, I was frustrated, and I took it out on you. And that's not fair."

Grace looked at him, her heart breaking at the sincerity in his voice. She knew that he was telling the truth, that he hadn't meant to hurt her, but the pain was still there, a wound that hadn't yet healed.

"I'm sorry too, Ethan," she said softly, her voice trembling. "I shouldn't have said the things I said either. I was hurt, and I lashed out, and I know that wasn't right."

Ethan reached out and took her hand in his, his touch gentle and filled with love. "We both said things we didn't mean, Grace. But I don't want to let this tear us apart. I love you too much to let that happen."

Grace felt the tears well up in her eyes as she looked at him, the man she had given up so much for, the man she had chosen to build a life with. She knew that their love was worth fighting for, but she also knew that they couldn't move forward until they had truly forgiven each other.

"I love you too, Ethan," she whispered, her voice filled with emotion. "But I don't know how to get past this. How do we move forward when there's so much hurt between us?"

Ethan looked at her, his expression filled with determination. "We forgive each other, Grace. We let go of the hurt and the anger, and we choose to forgive. Because that's what love is. It's not about never hurting each other. It's about choosing to forgive when we do."

Grace nodded, her heart swelling with love for him. She knew that he was right. Love couldn't thrive in a place where resentment and anger festered. It needed forgiveness to grow, to heal, to move forward.

"Okay," she said softly, squeezing his hand. "I choose to forgive you, Ethan. And I hope you can forgive me too."

Ethan's eyes filled with tears as he pulled her into his arms, holding her close. "I forgive you, Grace. And I promise that I'll do everything I can to make things right between us."

They sat there, wrapped in each other's embrace, the weight of the conflict that had come between them slowly lifting. It wasn't an instant fix; the hurt was still there, but the choice to forgive was the first step in healing that hurt.

As they held each other, Grace felt a sense of peace begin to settle over her. She knew that the road ahead wouldn't be easy, that there would be more challenges and more conflicts, but she also knew that as long as they were willing to forgive each other, their love would endure.

In the days that followed, Grace and Ethan made a conscious effort to rebuild the trust that had been shaken by their argument. They talked more, listened more, and took the time to really understand each other's needs and feelings. It wasn't always easy—old habits die hard, and there were moments when they both slipped back into patterns of behavior that had caused their conflict in the first place. But each time, they reminded themselves of the promise they had made to each other—to forgive, to let go, and to move forward.

One evening, as they sat together on the couch, Ethan took Grace's hand and looked at her, his expression serious.

"I've been thinking a lot about what happened between us," he said softly. "About why we got to that point, and how we can make sure it doesn't happen again."

Grace nodded, her heart pounding in her chest. She had been thinking about it too, and she knew that they needed to address the root of their issues if they were going to truly move forward.

"I think," Ethan continued, his voice steady, "that we need to make more time for each other. I know I've been spending a lot of time at work, and I know that's been hard on you. But I don't want you to feel like you're second place in my life, because you're not. You're the most important person to me, Grace, and I need to start showing you that."

Grace felt a lump form in her throat as she listened to his words. She had been so afraid that he didn't see how much his absence was affecting her, but hearing him acknowledge it gave her hope.

"I appreciate that, Ethan," she said softly. "And I know that your work is important too. I don't want you to give up something that means so much to you. But I do need to feel like we're in this together, that we're both making an effort to keep our relationship strong."

Ethan nodded, his expression filled with determination. "We are in this together, Grace. And I'm committed to making sure that you never feel like you're alone in this. I want us to make time for each other, to do things that we both enjoy, to connect in ways that go beyond just being in the same room."

Grace smiled, feeling a sense of warmth and love fill her heart. "I'd like that too, Ethan. I think that's exactly what we need."

And so they began to make changes, small at first, but meaningful. Ethan made a point to leave work on time more often, and they started spending their evenings together, whether it was cooking dinner, taking a walk, or simply sitting on the couch and talking about their day. They rediscovered the joy of being in each other's company, of sharing the little moments that made up their life together.

But more than that, they made a commitment to be more forgiving, not just in the big moments, but in the small ones too. When one of them said something hurtful or acted out of frustration, they chose to forgive quickly, to let go of the anger and resentment before it had a chance to take root. It wasn't always easy—sometimes the hurt was deeper than they realized—but they kept coming back to the promise they had made to each other, the promise to forgive.

One evening, as they sat on the porch, watching the sun set over the city, Grace leaned her head on Ethan's shoulder and sighed contentedly.

"I think we're getting better at this," she said softly, her voice filled with contentment.

Ethan smiled, his hand gently stroking her hair. "I think so too. It's not always easy, but I think we're learning how to love each other better."

Grace nodded, feeling a sense of peace wash over her. "I think forgiveness has a lot to do with that. It's like we're choosing to love each other more by choosing to forgive."

Ethan kissed the top of her head, his heart swelling with love for her. "You're right, Grace. Forgiveness is a big part of love. It's about letting go of the hurt and choosing to see the good in each other. And I think that's something we're going to keep learning, for the rest of our lives."

Grace smiled, feeling a sense of hope and joy that she hadn't felt in a long time. "I'm okay with that," she said softly. "As long as we're learning together."

And as the sun dipped below the horizon, casting a warm, golden light over the city, Grace and Ethan knew that their love had been strengthened by the trials they had faced. They had learned that love wasn't just about the good times, but about choosing to forgive, to let go, and to move forward together. And in that, they found a love that was deeper, stronger, and more enduring than they had ever imagined.

Theological Reflection

FORGIVENESS IS A CENTRAL theme in the Christian faith, and it is essential to any loving relationship. In Ephesians 4:32, the Apostle Paul urges us to "be kind and compassionate to one another, forgiving each other, just as in Christ God forgave you." This verse reminds us that forgiveness is not just a one-time act, but a continual practice that is rooted in the love and grace we have received from God.

In the story of Grace and Ethan, we see the power of forgiveness at work in their relationship. Their conflict was painful, and the words they exchanged left deep wounds. But it was through the act of forgiveness that they were able to heal those wounds and move forward together. They chose to let go of the hurt and anger, to extend grace to each other, and to rebuild the trust that had been shaken.

Forgiveness is not always easy. It requires humility, compassion, and a willingness to let go of the need to be right. It means choosing to see the person we love through the lens of grace, to understand that we are all flawed and in need of forgiveness. And it means trusting that God's love and forgiveness are sufficient to heal even the deepest wounds.

As we reflect on the role of forgiveness in love, we are reminded that our ability to forgive others is rooted in the forgiveness we have received from God. Just as Christ forgave us, we are called to forgive each other. It is through this act of forgiveness that we are able to experience the fullness of love, to build relationships that are strong, healthy, and enduring.

May we always strive to be kind and compassionate to one another, to forgive as we have been forgiven, and to build our relationships on a foundation of love and grace. And may we find the strength to forgive, even when it is difficult, knowing that in doing so, we are reflecting the heart of God and experiencing the true power of love.

Chapter 6: Love's Patience

The early morning light filtered through the trees, casting dappled shadows across the quiet path that wound through the park. The world was just beginning to wake, the air still crisp with the lingering chill of night. Birds sang softly in the branches above, their melodies a gentle reminder of the new day's promise. Grace Elliott walked slowly, her steps measured and deliberate, as she took in the serene beauty around her. But despite the peacefulness of the morning, her heart was anything but calm.

For months now, Grace had been grappling with a deep sense of restlessness. It was as if she were standing at a crossroads, knowing that a decision needed to be made, but unsure of which path to take. Her relationship with Ethan Matthews, the man she loved with all her heart, had been growing stronger every day. They had faced trials together, learned the art of forgiveness, and built a love that was deep and abiding. Yet, there was one thing they hadn't yet done, and it was the thing that weighed most heavily on her mind.

Marriage.

It was the natural next step in their relationship, something they had talked about many times. Grace had always imagined herself walking down the aisle, dressed in white, toward the man she loved, ready to make a lifelong commitment. But as the months passed and their conversations about the future remained just that—conversations—Grace began to wonder if Ethan was ever going to take that final step.

It wasn't that she doubted his love for her. Ethan had shown her time and again how much she meant to him. He was thoughtful, caring, and always there when she needed him. But despite all of this, he hadn't yet proposed, and that uncertainty gnawed at her.

Grace knew that patience was a virtue, one that she had always prided herself on possessing. But as the days turned into weeks and the weeks into months, her patience began to wear thin. She found herself growing frustrated, wondering why Ethan seemed so hesitant to move forward. Was he unsure about their future? Did he have doubts about their relationship that he hadn't shared with her?

The questions swirled in her mind, feeding the restlessness that had taken hold of her heart. She wanted so badly to trust in God's timing, to believe that everything would happen when it was meant to, but the waiting was becoming more and more difficult.

As Grace reached the edge of the park, she found herself standing before a small pond, the water still and reflective, mirroring the sky above. She paused, taking in the quiet beauty of the scene, and let out a long sigh. She knew she needed to talk to someone about what she was feeling, to get some perspective before her frustration consumed her.

She pulled out her phone and scrolled through her contacts, stopping when she found the name she was looking for. Rachel, her best friend, had always been a source of wisdom and comfort. If anyone could help her make sense of what she was feeling, it was Rachel.

After a few rings, Rachel's cheerful voice came through the line. "Hey, Grace! What's up?"

Grace smiled at the sound of her friend's voice, feeling a small measure of relief. "Hey, Rachel. I hope I'm not interrupting anything."

"Not at all," Rachel replied. "I was just about to make some coffee. Want to come over and join me?"

Grace hesitated for a moment, then nodded, even though Rachel couldn't see her. "Yeah, I'd like that. I need to talk to you about something."

"Uh-oh, that sounds serious," Rachel said, a note of concern creeping into her voice. "Come on over. I'll have the coffee ready by the time you get here."

Grace thanked her and ended the call, slipping her phone back into her pocket as she turned and made her way out of the park. Rachel's apartment was only a short walk away, and as she headed in that direction, Grace tried to calm the storm of emotions swirling inside her. She knew that talking to Rachel would help, but she also knew that she needed to be honest with herself about what she was feeling.

When she arrived at Rachel's apartment, she found the door slightly ajar, the aroma of freshly brewed coffee wafting out into the hallway. She knocked lightly on the door before pushing it open and stepping inside.

"Grace! Come on in!" Rachel called from the kitchen, her voice warm and inviting.

Grace followed the sound of her friend's voice and found Rachel pouring coffee into two mugs. The kitchen was cozy, filled with the comforting smell of coffee and the soft glow of morning light streaming through the windows.

"Here you go," Rachel said, handing Grace one of the mugs before leading her to the small dining table in the corner of the room. "Now, tell me what's going on."

Grace took a sip of her coffee, savoring the warmth as it spread through her, before setting the mug down and meeting Rachel's gaze. "It's about Ethan," she began, her voice hesitant. "I've been feeling... I don't know, frustrated lately. We've been together for so long now, and we've talked about getting married, but he still hasn't proposed. And I guess I'm starting to wonder if he ever will."

Rachel listened quietly, her expression thoughtful as Grace continued. "I know I need to be patient, to trust in God's timing, but it's hard, Rachel. I love him so much, and I want to spend the rest of my life with him. But the waiting is getting to me."

Rachel reached across the table and took Grace's hand, giving it a reassuring squeeze. "I get it, Grace. Waiting is never easy, especially when it's something as important as this. But have you talked to Ethan about how you're feeling?"

Grace shook her head, feeling a pang of guilt. "Not really. I've mentioned marriage a few times, but I haven't told him how much the waiting is bothering me. I don't want to pressure him or make him feel like he has to propose just because I'm getting impatient."

Rachel nodded, understanding. "I think it's important to be honest with him, Grace. You're not pressuring him by sharing your feelings. If anything, it might help him understand where you're coming from. But I also think you're right about trusting in God's timing. Sometimes, things happen when we least expect them, and maybe there's a reason for the wait that we can't see right now."

Grace sighed, knowing that Rachel was right. She needed to talk to Ethan, to be honest about her feelings, but she also needed to find a way to be patient, to trust that everything would happen when it was meant to.

"I know you're right," Grace said softly. "I just wish I knew what God's plan was, you know? It would make the waiting a lot easier."

Rachel smiled, her eyes filled with understanding. "I know, Grace. But that's where faith comes in. We have to trust that God's plan is perfect, even when we don't understand it. And in the meantime, we can choose to be patient, to be kind, and to love each other through the waiting."

Grace nodded, feeling a sense of peace begin to settle over her. She knew that Rachel was right—patience was an essential part of love, and it was something she needed to cultivate in her relationship with Ethan. It wouldn't be easy, but she was willing to try.

"Thanks, Rachel," Grace said, giving her friend a grateful smile. "You always know what to say."

Rachel returned the smile, her eyes warm with affection. "That's what friends are for. And remember, Grace, you're not alone in this. God's with you every step of the way, and so am I."

They finished their coffee, chatting about lighter topics as Grace's heart began to feel lighter. She knew that she had a conversation with Ethan ahead of her, but she also knew that she could face it with honesty and patience.

Later that evening, Grace found herself standing in the kitchen, preparing dinner as she waited for Ethan to come home. The sun was setting, casting a warm golden light across the room, and the soft sound of music played in the background. But despite the peacefulness of the moment, Grace's heart was racing with anticipation. She knew that tonight, she needed to talk to Ethan about what had been weighing on her heart.

When she heard the sound of the front door opening, Grace took a deep breath, trying to steady her nerves. She could hear Ethan's footsteps as he made his way into the kitchen, and when he appeared in the doorway, she turned to greet him with a smile.

"Hey," she said softly, her voice betraying the nervousness she felt.

Ethan returned her smile, though there was a hint of weariness in his expression. "Hey, Grace. How was your day?"

"It was good," Grace replied, setting down the knife she had been using to chop vegetables. "I spent some time with Rachel this morning, and then I came home to get dinner ready."

Ethan nodded, crossing the room to wrap his arms around her from behind. "That sounds nice. I'm glad you got to spend some time with her."

Grace leaned into his embrace, feeling a sense of comfort in his presence. But she knew that she couldn't let the moment pass without addressing what had been on her mind.

"Ethan," she began, her voice soft, "there's something I've been wanting to talk to you about."

Ethan's arms tightened around her slightly, and she could feel him tense. "What is it?" he asked, his voice cautious.

Grace turned in his arms so that she was facing him, looking up into his eyes as she tried to find the right words

. "I've been feeling... a little restless lately," she admitted, her voice trembling slightly. "We've talked about our future, about getting married, but we haven't taken any steps toward making that a reality. And I guess I'm starting to wonder why."

Ethan's expression softened, and he reached up to gently brush a strand of hair behind her ear. "Grace, I love you more than anything. And I do want to marry you. But I've been waiting for the right time, the right moment to make it special. I didn't want to rush it."

Grace felt her heart swell with love for him, but she also felt a pang of sadness. "I appreciate that, Ethan. I really do. But I need you to know that the waiting has been hard for me. I've been trying to be patient, to trust that everything will happen when it's meant to, but I can't help feeling anxious about it."

Ethan's eyes filled with understanding, and he took her hands in his, squeezing them gently. "I'm sorry, Grace. I didn't realize how much the waiting was affecting you. I thought I was doing the right thing by waiting for the perfect moment, but I see now that it's been causing you pain. That's the last thing I want."

Grace felt a tear slip down her cheek, and she quickly wiped it away. "I'm not trying to rush you, Ethan. I just... I need to know that we're on the same page, that we're moving forward together."

Ethan nodded, his gaze steady as he looked into her eyes. "We are, Grace. I promise you, we are. And I want you to know that I'm committed to our future, to building a life together. I don't want you to doubt that, not for a second."

Grace felt a wave of relief wash over her, and she let out a breath she hadn't realized she was holding. "Thank you, Ethan. That means so much to me."

Ethan pulled her into his arms, holding her close as he pressed a kiss to the top of her head. "I love you, Grace. And I want you to know that I've been planning something special. I didn't want to tell you before because I wanted it to be a surprise, but I think you need to know now."

Grace looked up at him, her heart racing. "What do you mean?"

Ethan smiled, his eyes twinkling with a mixture of excitement and love. "I've been planning to propose, Grace. I've been working with a jeweler to create a custom ring, something that's as unique and beautiful as you are. I wanted it to be perfect, but I see now that I should have shared this with you sooner."

Grace's breath caught in her throat, and she felt a rush of emotion overwhelm her. "Ethan... I don't know what to say."

"You don't have to say anything," Ethan said softly, his voice filled with love. "Just know that I've always been committed to you, and I always will be. I wanted to make sure everything was just right, but I see now that what matters most is that we're together, that we're moving forward as a team."

Grace felt the tears streaming down her face, but this time, they were tears of joy and relief. "I love you, Ethan. And I'm so sorry for doubting you. I just... I needed to know that we were on the same page."

"We are, Grace," Ethan assured her, his voice steady and filled with conviction. "And we're going to spend the rest of our lives building something beautiful together."

Grace leaned up and pressed a soft kiss to his lips, feeling the weight of her worries lift from her shoulders. She knew that the journey they were on was far from over, but she also knew that they were moving forward together, with love and patience guiding their way.

The days that followed were filled with a renewed sense of hope and excitement. Grace and Ethan continued to build their life together, focusing on their relationship and the love that had brought them this far. They talked more openly about their future, about their hopes and dreams, and they made plans for the life they wanted to create.

But most importantly, they learned to be patient with each other. They understood that love wasn't something that could be rushed, that it needed time to grow and deepen. They embraced the waiting, knowing that it was a part of their journey, and that it would only make their love stronger.

One evening, as they sat on the porch, watching the sun set over the city, Grace leaned her head on Ethan's shoulder and sighed contentedly.

"I think we're getting better at this," she said softly, her voice filled with contentment.

Ethan smiled, his hand gently stroking her hair. "I think so too. It's not always easy, but I think we're learning how to love each other better."

Grace nodded, feeling a sense of warmth and love fill her heart. "I think patience has a lot to do with that. It's like we're choosing to love each other more by choosing to be patient."

Ethan kissed the top of her head, his heart swelling with love for her. "You're right, Grace. Patience is a big part of love. It's about giving each other the time and space we need, and trusting that everything will happen when it's meant to."

Grace smiled, feeling a sense of hope and joy that she hadn't felt in a long time. "I'm okay with that," she said softly. "As long as we're learning together."

And as the sun dipped below the horizon, casting a warm, golden light over the city, Grace and Ethan knew that their love had been strengthened by the patience they had shown each other. They had learned that love wasn't just about the good times, but about choosing to be patient, to trust, and to move forward together. And in that, they found a love that was deeper, stronger, and more enduring than they had ever imagined.

Theological Reflection

PATIENCE IS A CENTRAL virtue in the Christian faith, and it is essential to any loving relationship. In 1 Corinthians 13:4, the Apostle Paul reminds us that "Love is patient, love is kind." This verse highlights the importance of patience in love, and it reminds us that true love is not something that can be rushed or forced. It is something that grows and deepens over time, and it requires patience, understanding, and trust.

In the story of Grace and Ethan, we see the power of patience at work in their relationship. The waiting was difficult, and it tested their love in ways they hadn't expected. But through the trial of waiting, they learned to be patient with each other, to trust in God's timing, and to embrace the journey they were on.

Patience in love is about more than just waiting for the right moment. It is about giving each other the time and space we need to grow, to heal, and to build something beautiful together. It is about trusting that everything will happen when it is meant to, and that God's plan is perfect, even when we don't understand it.

As we reflect on the role of patience in love, we are reminded that our ability to be patient with others is rooted in the patience and love we have received from God. Just as God is patient with us, we are called to be patient with each other. It is through this patience that we are able to build relationships that are strong, healthy, and enduring.

May we always strive to be patient with those we love, to trust in God's timing, and to build our relationships on a foundation of love, patience, and understanding. And may we find the strength to be patient, even when it is difficult, knowing that in doing so, we are reflecting the heart of God and experiencing the true power of love.

Chapter 7: The Gift of Grace

The morning sun filtered gently through the curtains, casting a warm, golden light across the room. The soft hum of city life buzzed outside the window, but inside, the apartment was still and quiet. Grace Elliott sat at the small dining table, her hands wrapped around a steaming mug of tea, but her mind was far from the peaceful morning scene. Her thoughts were heavy, swirling with the weight of last night's events—a night that had tested the strength of her love and the depth of her forgiveness.

Ethan Matthews, the man she loved more than life itself, had been struggling for weeks. He had always been her rock, the one she could lean on when life's challenges seemed too great to bear. But recently, Grace had noticed a change in him—an unease that he couldn't seem to shake, a darkness that clouded his usually bright and optimistic spirit. At first, she had thought it was just the stress of his demanding job at the hospital. But as time went on, it became clear that something deeper was at play.

Ethan had become more withdrawn, his usual warmth replaced by a cold distance that Grace couldn't understand. He was quick to anger, his patience worn thin by the invisible burden he carried. Grace had tried to reach out to him, to offer her support and understanding, but her efforts were often met with frustration and resistance. The man she loved seemed to be slipping away from her, and she didn't know how to bring him back.

Last night had been the breaking point.

Ethan had come home late, his face drawn and weary, his eyes shadowed with exhaustion. Grace had been waiting for him, hoping to talk, to find a way to bridge the growing gap between them. But when she had gently asked him how he was feeling, Ethan had exploded, his words harsh and biting.

"Why do you keep asking me that, Grace?" he had snapped, his voice laced with irritation. "I'm fine. I'm just tired. Can't you understand that?"

Grace had been taken aback by the sharpness of his tone, her heart aching at the way he had looked at her—like she was an inconvenience, a burden he couldn't bear. "I'm just worried about you, Ethan," she had replied softly, trying to keep the hurt out of her voice. "I can see that something's been bothering you, and I want to help."

But Ethan had only grown more agitated, his frustration boiling over. "I don't need your help, Grace! I just need some space, some time to figure things out on my own. Why can't you just leave me alone?"

The words had cut deep, and Grace had felt tears well up in her eyes. But before she could respond, Ethan had turned and stormed out of the apartment, slamming the door behind him. The sound had echoed through the empty room, leaving Grace standing there, stunned and heartbroken.

She had spent the rest of the night sitting on the couch, staring at the door, waiting for him to come back. But he hadn't. The hours had ticked by slowly, the silence of the apartment growing heavier with each passing moment. By the time the first light of dawn had begun to creep through the windows, Grace had realized that Ethan wasn't coming home that night.

Now, as she sat at the table, the events of the night replaying in her mind, Grace felt a deep sense of sorrow settle over her. She loved Ethan with all her heart, but she didn't know how to help him, how to reach him when he was so determined to push her away. She felt helpless, caught between her desire to be there for him and the pain of his rejection.

But even in her sorrow, Grace knew that she couldn't give up on him. She had made a commitment to love him, in good times and bad, and she wasn't going to let him face this darkness alone. She knew that he was hurting, that something was eating away at him from the inside, and she was determined to stand by his side, no matter how difficult it might be.

She took a deep breath, closing her eyes as she offered a silent prayer. "God, please give me the strength to be there for Ethan, to love him even when he pushes me away. Help me to extend grace to him, just as You have extended grace to me. I know that Your grace is sufficient, and that Your power is made perfect in weakness. Please, help me to trust in that, and to be a source of love and light for Ethan during this dark time."

As she finished her prayer, Grace felt a sense of peace begin to wash over her, a reminder that she wasn't facing this challenge alone. God was with her, guiding her, giving her the strength she needed to love Ethan through this difficult season.

Just as she was about to get up from the table, the sound of the front door opening caught her attention. Her heart leapt into her throat as she turned to see Ethan step into the apartment, his clothes rumpled and his eyes bloodshot. He looked exhausted, defeated, as if the weight of the world was pressing down on him.

"Ethan," Grace said softly, rising from her seat. "You're home."

Ethan looked at her, his expression filled with a mixture of shame and sorrow. "Grace, I'm so sorry," he said, his voice hoarse. "I shouldn't have spoken to you the way I did. I shouldn't have left like that."

Grace felt tears prick at the corners of her eyes as she took a step toward him. "It's okay, Ethan. I understand. You're going through something, and I know it's not easy."

Ethan shook his head, his eyes filled with regret. "No, it's not okay. I hurt you, Grace, and that's the last thing I ever wanted to do. I don't know what's wrong with me. I feel like I'm losing control, like I'm drowning and I can't find my way out."

Grace reached out and took his hands in hers, squeezing them gently. "You're not alone, Ethan. I'm here with you, and I'm not going anywhere. Whatever you're going through, we'll face it together."

Ethan's eyes filled with tears as he looked at her, his voice trembling with emotion. "How can you still love me after the way I treated you? I don't deserve your forgiveness, Grace."

Grace's heart ached at the pain in his voice, but she knew that this was a moment to extend grace, to show him that love was not dependent on perfection, but on commitment and compassion.

"Ethan, love isn't about deserving," she said softly. "It's about choosing to be there for each other, even when it's hard. We all have moments of weakness, times when we fall short. But that's when grace comes in. God's grace is sufficient for us, even in our weakest moments. And I want to extend that grace to you, just as God has extended it to me."

Ethan's tears spilled over as he pulled Grace into his arms, holding her tightly. "I don't know what I did to deserve you, Grace, but I'm so grateful for you. I don't want to lose you."

Grace wrapped her arms around him, feeling the tension in his body begin to ease as he held her. "You're not going to lose me, Ethan. I'm here, and I'm not going anywhere. We'll get through this together."

They stood there for a long time, wrapped in each other's embrace, the weight of the previous night's pain slowly lifting as they allowed grace to fill the space between them. Grace knew that this wasn't the end of their challenges, that there would be more difficult moments ahead. But she also knew that they had taken an important step forward, a step toward healing and restoration.

In the days that followed, Grace and Ethan began to rebuild the trust that had been shaken by the events of that night. It wasn't an easy process—there were still moments of tension, times when old wounds were reopened—but they were committed to working through it together, to extending grace to each other in their moments of weakness.

Ethan opened up to Grace about the struggles he had been facing at work, the pressures and expectations that had been weighing heavily on him. He admitted that he had been bottling up his emotions, trying to handle everything on his own, but that it had only led to more stress and frustration. Grace listened with compassion, offering her support and understanding, and encouraging him to take time for himself, to rest and recharge.

Grace, in turn, shared her own feelings of helplessness and fear, the worry that she wasn't enough to help him through this difficult time. Ethan reassured her that she was more than enough, that her love and support were what kept him going, even on the darkest days.

Through these conversations, they began to find a new rhythm in their relationship, one that was built on honesty, vulnerability, and grace. They learned to lean on each other, to share their burdens, and to trust that they could face anything as long as they were together.

One evening, as they sat on the couch, the soft glow of the fireplace casting a warm light across the room, Ethan took Grace's hand and looked into her eyes.

"Grace," he began, his voice filled with emotion, "I want you to know how much I appreciate you. I know I haven't always made it easy, but your love and grace have been a lifeline for me. I don't know where I'd be without you."

Grace felt tears well up in her eyes as she squeezed his hand. "You don't have to thank me, Ethan. I love you, and that's what love does. It stands by you, even when things are hard."

Ethan nodded, his eyes filled with gratitude. "I know, but I still want you to know how much it means to me. I've been thinking a lot about what you said, about grace, and how it's not about deserving but about choosing to love each other through our weaknesses. That's what I want for us, Grace. I want us to always choose grace, to always choose love, no matter what."

Grace smiled, feeling a deep sense of peace settle over her. "I want that too, Ethan. And I believe that with God's grace, we can do it. We can build a love that's strong and enduring, one that reflects the grace and love that God has shown us."

Ethan leaned in and kissed her softly, his heart overflowing with love and gratitude for the woman beside him. As they sat together, wrapped in each other's arms, they knew that they had been given a gift—a gift of grace that had the power to heal, to restore, and to strengthen their love.

The weeks that followed were filled with moments of grace, small acts of kindness and love that helped to mend the wounds that had been inflicted. Grace and Ethan made a conscious effort to be more patient with each other, to listen with compassion, and to extend grace in moments of frustration or misunderstanding.

One evening, as they were preparing dinner together, Grace accidentally dropped a plate, sending it crashing to the floor. The sound of breaking glass echoed through the kitchen, and for a moment, Grace froze, her heart sinking.

"I'm so sorry, Ethan," she said quickly, bending down to pick up the pieces. "I didn't mean to—"

But before she could finish, Ethan was there, gently taking her hands and stopping her from cleaning up the mess. "It's okay, Grace," he said softly, his voice filled with warmth. "It's just a plate. We can replace it."

Grace looked up at him, her eyes filled with surprise and relief. In the past, a moment like this might have led to tension or frustration, but now, there was only understanding and grace.

Ethan smiled at her, his eyes twinkling with affection. "Let's clean this up together, and then we'll finish making dinner. No harm done."

As they worked together to clean up the broken pieces, Grace felt a sense of gratitude wash over her. It was such a small thing—a broken plate—but the way Ethan had responded showed her just how far they had come. They were learning to choose grace, to respond with love and understanding, even in the small moments.

Later that evening, as they sat down to dinner, Ethan reached across the table and took Grace's hand. "I know it's just a plate," he said with a smile, "but I want you to know that I'm committed to making grace a part of our everyday lives. I don't want us to sweat the small stuff. I want us to focus on what really matters—our love, our relationship, and the grace that God has given us."

Grace smiled, her heart swelling with love for him. "I love that, Ethan. And I'm committed to the same. I want us to always choose grace, to always choose love."

As they ate their meal, talking and laughing together, Grace felt a deep sense of peace and contentment. She knew that their journey wasn't over, that there would still be challenges and difficult moments ahead. But she also knew that they were stronger now, that they had been given the gift of grace—a gift that would sustain them, no matter what came their way.

Theological Reflection

GRACE IS A CENTRAL theme in the Christian faith, and it is essential to any loving relationship. In 2 Corinthians 12:9, the Apostle Paul writes, "But he said to me, 'My grace is sufficient for you, for my power is made perfect in weakness.'" This verse reminds us that God's grace is not just a one-time gift, but a continual source of strength and power, especially in our moments of weakness.

In the story of Grace and Ethan, we see the power of grace at work in their relationship. Their journey was filled with challenges, moments of weakness, and times when they hurt each other. But through it all, they learned to extend grace to each other, to forgive, and to choose love, even when it was difficult.

Grace is not about deserving—it is about choosing to love and forgive, even when the other person falls short. It is about recognizing our own weaknesses and trusting that God's grace is sufficient to carry us through. It is through grace that we are able to build relationships that are strong, healthy, and enduring.

As we reflect on the role of grace in love, we are reminded that our ability to extend grace to others is rooted in the grace we have received from God. Just as God's grace is sufficient for us, we are called to extend that grace to those we love. It is through this grace that we are able to experience the fullness of love, to build relationships that reflect the heart of God, and to find strength in our moments of weakness.

May we always strive to extend grace to those we love, to forgive as we have been forgiven, and to build our relationships on a foundation of love and grace. And may we find the strength to choose grace, even when it is difficult, knowing that in doing so, we are reflecting the heart of God and experiencing the true power of love.

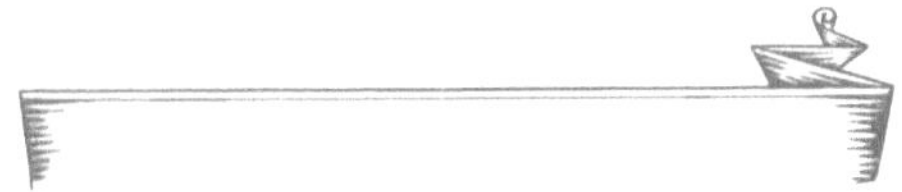

Chapter 8: Love's Kindness

The soft hum of city life surrounded Grace Elliott and Ethan Matthews as they walked hand in hand down the bustling streets of their neighborhood. It was a warm, sunny Saturday afternoon, and the city was alive with energy. Children played in the park, couples strolled by with their dogs, and the air was filled with the sound of laughter and conversation. It was the kind of day that seemed to glow with the promise of possibility, and yet, for Grace and Ethan, it was the quiet, unspoken moments between them that made the day truly special.

Their relationship had weathered many storms, from the early days of long-distance love to the more recent trials that had tested their patience and faith. But through it all, they had learned that the foundation of their love was built on something much deeper than passion or excitement—it was built on kindness, the small, everyday acts of consideration and care that reminded them both of their commitment to each other.

As they walked, Grace couldn't help but reflect on how much their relationship had grown and matured over the past year. They had faced challenges that might have torn other couples apart, but instead, those challenges had drawn them closer together. And now, as they walked side by side, the simplicity of their love felt like the greatest blessing of all.

Ethan glanced over at Grace, a soft smile playing on his lips as he squeezed her hand gently. "What are you thinking about?" he asked, his voice filled with affection.

Grace returned his smile, feeling a warmth spread through her chest at the sound of his voice. "I was just thinking about us," she replied softly. "About how far we've come, and how much we've grown together."

Ethan nodded, his expression thoughtful. "We have come a long way, haven't we? I think a lot of that has to do with the way we've learned to take care of each other, to show kindness in the small things."

Grace's heart swelled with love as she looked up at him. "I agree. It's the little things that make all the difference, isn't it? The way you bring me coffee in the morning, or the way you always listen when I've had a tough day... those things mean more to me than you'll ever know."

Ethan's smile widened, and he pulled her closer, wrapping his arm around her shoulders as they continued walking. "I feel the same way, Grace. The way you always know just what to say to make me feel better, or the way you leave those little notes in my lunch... those things remind me every day how lucky I am to have you in my life."

They walked in comfortable silence for a few moments, the sounds of the city fading into the background as they focused on each other. It was true—kindness had become the cornerstone of their relationship, the thing that had sustained them through the ups and downs of life. And it was a kindness that wasn't just about grand gestures or dramatic declarations of love, but about the quiet, consistent ways they showed each other that they cared.

As they approached a small café on the corner of the street, Ethan suddenly stopped, his gaze fixed on something ahead. "Look," he said softly, nodding toward the entrance of the café.

Grace followed his gaze and saw an elderly man sitting on a bench just outside the café, a cup of coffee in his hands and a distant look in his eyes. He was dressed in a worn, faded coat, his hair thin and gray, and there was a sense of loneliness about him that tugged at Grace's heart.

Ethan's expression softened as he watched the man, and he turned to Grace with a look of quiet determination. "Let's get him something to eat," he suggested. "I think he could use a little kindness today."

Grace's heart swelled with love for Ethan, and she nodded, her smile warm and approving. "I think that's a wonderful idea."

They walked into the café together, the door chiming softly as they entered. The warm, inviting scent of freshly brewed coffee and baked goods filled the air, and the atmosphere was cozy and welcoming. They approached the counter, where a friendly barista greeted them with a smile.

"What can I get for you?" the barista asked, her tone cheerful.

Ethan glanced at the menu for a moment before turning back to the barista. "We'd like to get a sandwich and a coffee for the gentleman sitting outside," he said. "And we'll have two coffees for ourselves, please."

The barista's smile widened, and she nodded. "Of course. That's very kind of you."

As the barista prepared their order, Grace looked over at Ethan, her heart filled with admiration. It was moments like this that reminded her why she had fallen in love with him in the first place. Ethan had always had a generous spirit, a deep-seated kindness that shone through in everything he did. And it was that kindness that had drawn her to him, that had made her believe in the possibility of a love that was truly selfless.

When their order was ready, they took the sandwich and coffee outside to the elderly man. As they approached, the man looked up, his eyes filled with surprise as he saw them standing before him.

"Hello," Ethan said warmly, holding out the sandwich and coffee. "We thought you might like something to eat."

The man's eyes widened, and for a moment, he seemed at a loss for words. Then, slowly, a smile spread across his face, and he reached out to take the food with trembling hands. "Thank you," he said softly, his voice filled with gratitude. "You didn't have to do this."

Ethan shook his head, his expression kind. "It's our pleasure. We just wanted to do something nice for you."

The man nodded, his eyes misting over with emotion. "It's been a long time since someone's shown me this kind of kindness. You've made my day."

Grace felt tears prick at the corners of her eyes as she watched the exchange, her heart swelling with love and compassion. "We're glad we could help," she said gently. "Take care of yourself, okay?"

The man nodded again, his smile still in place as he looked at them both. "I will. Thank you, both of you."

As they walked away, Grace slipped her hand into Ethan's, squeezing it gently. "That was a beautiful thing you just did," she said softly, her voice filled with admiration.

Ethan smiled, his eyes twinkling with warmth. "It was just a small thing, but I think small acts of kindness can make a big difference. It's something I've been thinking about a lot lately—how important it is to be kind, even in the little things."

Grace nodded, her heart filled with love and gratitude for the man beside her. "I think you're right. Kindness is what makes love real, isn't it? It's what keeps love alive."

Ethan looked at her, his expression serious and thoughtful. "It is. And I want to make sure that I'm always showing you that kind of kindness, Grace. I don't ever want you to doubt how much I care about you."

Grace felt her eyes well up with tears as she looked at him, her heart overflowing with love. "I never have, Ethan. You've always shown me kindness, in everything you do. And I hope I've done the same for you."

"You have," Ethan said softly, his voice filled with emotion. "More than you know."

They continued their walk, their hands intertwined, the warmth of their connection palpable in the air around them. As they walked, Grace couldn't help but reflect on the importance of kindness in their relationship. It was the thread that had woven their lives together, the thing that had sustained them through the challenges they had faced. And it was a kindness that wasn't just about grand gestures, but about the small, everyday acts that reminded them both of their love.

Over the next few weeks, Grace and Ethan continued to focus on the small acts of kindness that had become such an integral part of their relationship. They made a conscious effort to show each other kindness in the little things—leaving sweet notes for each other, surprising each other with small gifts, and taking the time to really listen and be present for each other.

One evening, after a long day at work, Grace came home to find the apartment filled with the warm, inviting scent of her favorite meal—lasagna. She smiled as she set down her bag and made her way to the kitchen, where she found Ethan standing at the stove, stirring a pot of sauce.

"Hey, you," she said, her voice filled with affection. "What's all this?"

Ethan turned to her with a smile, his eyes twinkling with warmth. "I thought you could use a nice, home-cooked meal after the day you've had. I know you've been working hard lately, and I wanted to do something nice for you."

Grace's heart swelled with love as she walked over to him, wrapping her arms around his waist from behind. "You're amazing, you know that?"

Ethan chuckled, turning around to pull her into a hug. "I'm just trying to take care of you, Grace. You do so much for me, and I want to make sure you know how much I appreciate you."

Grace rested her head against his chest, feeling a deep sense of contentment wash over her. "I do know, Ethan. And I hope you know how much I appreciate you too."

Ethan kissed the top of her head, his arms tightening around her. "I do, Grace. I really do."

They sat down to dinner together, the warmth of their connection filling the room. As they ate, they talked about their day, sharing stories and laughing together. It was a simple, ordinary evening, but it was filled with the kind of love that was built on a foundation of kindness and care.

After dinner, they curled up on the couch together, watching a movie and enjoying each other's company. As they sat there, Grace couldn't help but reflect on how much she had come to value these small, quiet moments with Ethan. It wasn't about the grand gestures or the big, dramatic declarations of love—it was about the everyday acts of kindness that reminded her of just how much she was loved.

As the weeks turned into months, Grace and Ethan continued to build their relationship on the foundation of kindness they had established. They learned to be patient with each other, to offer grace in moments of frustration, and to show kindness in the small, everyday things.

One day, as they were out running errands together, they came across a young mother struggling to carry her groceries while holding onto a wiggling toddler. Without hesitation, Ethan stepped forward to offer his help, carrying the heavy bags to her car while Grace entertained the child with a gentle smile and a few playful gestures.

"Thank you so much," the mother said, her voice filled with gratitude as she buckled her child into the car seat. "I don't know what I would have done without your help."

Ethan smiled, his eyes warm with kindness. "It was our pleasure. We're happy to help."

As they walked away, Grace looked up at Ethan, her heart filled with admiration. "You're always thinking of others, Ethan. It's one of the things I love most about you."

Ethan looked down at her, his expression thoughtful. "I think it's important to be kind, Grace. It's something I've always believed in. You never know what someone else is going through, and a little kindness can go a long way."

Grace nodded, feeling a deep sense of gratitude for the man beside her. "It's true. Kindness is what makes the world a better place. And it's what makes our love so special."

They continued their day, running their errands and enjoying each other's company. But even as they went about their tasks, the theme of kindness remained at the forefront of their minds. It was something they both valued deeply, something that had become a guiding principle in their relationship.

Later that evening, as they sat down to dinner, Grace looked across the table at Ethan, her heart swelling with love and gratitude. "I've been thinking a lot about kindness lately," she said softly, her voice filled with emotion. "About how important it is in our relationship, and how much it's helped us grow closer."

Ethan nodded, his expression serious and thoughtful. "I've been thinking about it too. Kindness is what makes love real, isn't it? It's what keeps us connected, even when things get tough."

Grace smiled, her eyes misting over with emotion. "It is. And I'm so grateful that we've built our relationship on that foundation. It's what makes our love so strong."

Ethan reached across the table and took her hand, squeezing it gently. "I'm grateful too, Grace. I think kindness is what's going to carry us through, no matter what life throws our way."

As they sat there, holding hands and sharing a quiet moment of connection, Grace felt a deep sense of peace and contentment. She knew that their relationship wasn't perfect, that there would still be challenges and difficult moments ahead. But she also knew that they had built something truly special—a love that was rooted in kindness, a love that would endure.

Theological Reflection

KINDNESS IS A CENTRAL virtue in the Christian faith, and it is essential to any loving relationship. Proverbs 19:22 reminds us that "What is desired in a man is kindness." This verse highlights the importance of kindness in our interactions with others, and it reminds us that true love is not just about grand gestures or dramatic declarations—it is about the small, everyday acts of kindness that build trust, connection, and intimacy.

In the story of Grace and Ethan, we see the power of kindness at work in their relationship. Their love is strengthened by the small acts of kindness they show each other—the thoughtful gestures, the words of encouragement, the willingness to help others in need. These acts of kindness are not just about making the other person feel good—they are about building a foundation of trust and love that can withstand the challenges of life.

Kindness in love is about more than just being nice—it is about being considerate, compassionate, and selfless. It is about putting the needs of others before our own, and about recognizing that love is not just about what we say, but about what we do. It is through kindness that we are able to build relationships that are strong, healthy, and enduring.

As we reflect on the role of kindness in love, we are reminded that our ability to be kind to others is rooted in the kindness we have received from God. Just as God's kindness leads us to repentance and transformation, our kindness toward others can lead to deeper connection, healing, and growth.

May we always strive to show kindness in our relationships, to be patient, understanding, and compassionate, and to build our relationships on a foundation of love and kindness. And may we find the strength to be kind, even when it is difficult, knowing that in doing so, we are reflecting the heart of God and experiencing the true power of love.

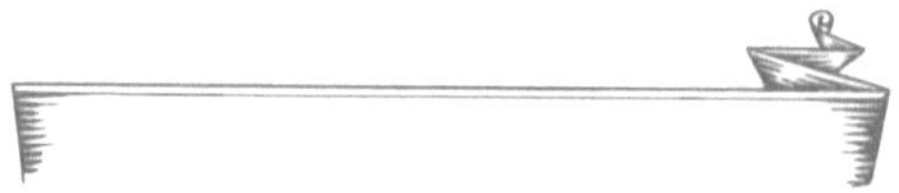

Chapter 9: Hope in Love

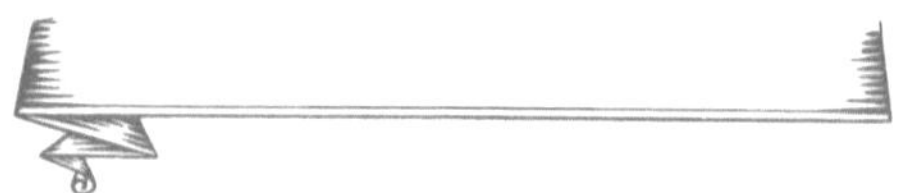

The late afternoon sun cast long shadows across the floor of the small apartment, the golden light filtering through the curtains and giving the room a warm, almost ethereal glow. Outside, the city hummed with life, the sounds of traffic and distant laughter a familiar backdrop to the day. But inside, the atmosphere was thick with unspoken tension, a weight that neither Grace Elliott nor Ethan Matthews could ignore any longer.

They sat across from each other at the small dining table, the remnants of their lunch still on their plates, untouched. The silence between them was heavy, filled with the uncertainty of the conversation they both knew they needed to have but were hesitant to start. It had been building for weeks now, a quiet undercurrent that had slowly grown stronger, pulling them toward a crossroads in their relationship.

Grace glanced across the table at Ethan, her heart aching at the sight of the worry etched on his face. She loved him more than anything, but she couldn't deny the knot of fear that had taken root in her chest. The uncertainty about their future had been gnawing at her, keeping her awake at night and leaving her feeling lost and adrift.

Ethan, too, had been struggling. His job at the hospital had become increasingly demanding, the pressures and responsibilities weighing heavily on his shoulders. The long hours and the emotional toll of his work had left him exhausted, and he knew that something had to give. But the question of what to do next, of how to move forward, loomed large in his mind, leaving him feeling trapped between his duty and his desire to build a life with Grace.

Finally, unable to bear the silence any longer, Grace spoke up, her voice soft but filled with the weight of her emotions. "Ethan, we need to talk about what's been happening... about us."

Ethan looked up at her, his eyes filled with a mixture of sadness and resignation. He had known this conversation was coming, and yet, he still wasn't sure he was ready to face it. "I know, Grace," he replied quietly. "I've been thinking about it too. There's a lot we need to figure out."

Grace nodded, her heart pounding in her chest as she gathered the courage to continue. "I love you, Ethan. I love the life we've built together, but I'm scared. I'm scared that we're not on the same page about our future. I'm scared that all this uncertainty is going to pull us apart."

Ethan's expression softened as he reached across the table to take her hand in his. "I love you too, Grace. And I don't want to lose what we have. But you're right—we need to figure out what's next for us. We need to talk about where we're going."

Grace felt a tear slip down her cheek as she looked at him, the fear and uncertainty she had been holding in finally breaking through. "I want to believe that we can get through this, that we can find a way forward together. But it feels like everything is so uncertain right now, like we're standing on the edge of something and I don't know if we're going to fall or fly."

Ethan squeezed her hand, his own heart heavy with the weight of their situation. "I know it feels that way, Grace. And I wish I could give you all the answers, but I don't have them. What I do know is that I don't want to face this uncertainty without you. Whatever happens, I want us to face it together."

Grace nodded, her heart aching with love and fear in equal measure. "But how do we do that, Ethan? How do we hold on to each other when everything feels so uncertain?"

Ethan was silent for a moment, his mind racing as he tried to find the right words. He had always been the one to fix things, to find solutions, but this was different. This wasn't something he could solve with a quick decision or a well-laid plan. This was about faith, about trust, about believing in something greater than the circumstances they found themselves in.

"I think we have to hold on to hope, Grace," he said finally, his voice steady but filled with emotion. "We have to believe that even in the midst of all this uncertainty, there's a plan for us, a purpose that we can't see yet. We have to trust that God's love is guiding us, even when the path isn't clear."

Grace looked at him, her eyes filled with tears, but also with a glimmer of something else—hope. "Do you really believe that, Ethan? Do you really believe that God's love is enough to carry us through this?"

Ethan nodded, his gaze unwavering as he met her eyes. "I do, Grace. I know it's hard, and I know it feels like we're walking in the dark right now, but I believe that God's love is the light that's guiding us. And I believe that as long as we hold on to that hope, we'll find our way."

Grace felt a surge of emotion wash over her as she listened to his words. She had always admired Ethan's strength, his ability to stay grounded even in the midst of chaos, but it was his faith that had drawn her to him in the first place. And now, as they faced this uncertainty together, she realized that it was that same faith that would see them through.

"You're right," she said softly, her voice trembling with emotion. "We have to hold on to hope. We have to believe that God has a plan for us, even if we can't see it right now."

Ethan smiled, a sense of relief washing over him as he saw the hope in her eyes. "We will, Grace. We'll hold on to each other, and we'll hold on to that hope. And we'll trust that God's love will guide us."

They sat in silence for a few moments, the weight of their conversation settling over them. But there was a sense of peace in the room now, a feeling that, despite the uncertainty, they were not alone in this. They had each other, and they had their faith, and that was enough.

The days that followed were not without their challenges. The uncertainty about their future still loomed large, and there were moments when the fear and doubt threatened to overwhelm them. But through it all, Grace and Ethan clung to the hope they had found in each other, the belief that God's love was guiding them through this difficult time.

They began to talk more openly about their fears, their hopes, and their dreams for the future. It wasn't always easy—there were moments of frustration, times when the uncertainty seemed too great to bear—but they learned to lean on each other, to find comfort in their shared faith and in the love that had brought them together.

One evening, as they sat on the couch together, Ethan turned to Grace with a thoughtful expression. "I've been thinking a lot about what you said, about the uncertainty we're facing," he began, his voice steady but serious. "And I've realized that a lot of my fear comes from not knowing what's next for us, from feeling like I have to have everything figured out right now."

Grace nodded, her own heart heavy with similar thoughts. "I feel the same way. I've been so focused on trying to control everything, on trying to make sure that we're on the right path, that I've forgotten to trust in God's plan."

Ethan reached out and took her hand, his gaze steady as he looked into her eyes. "I think we need to let go of that need for control, Grace. I think we need to focus on what we can control—how we treat each other, how we support each other—and trust that God will take care of the rest."

Grace felt a sense of relief wash over her as she listened to his words. She had been carrying the weight of that need for control for so long, and it had only added to her anxiety and fear. But now, as she looked at Ethan, she realized that he was right. They couldn't control the future, but they could control how they faced it together.

"You're right," she said softly, her voice filled with emotion. "We need to let go of that need for control and trust that God's love will guide us. We need to focus on the love we have for each other and let that be our anchor."

Ethan smiled, a sense of peace settling over him as he heard her words. "Exactly. And I think that's what hope is all about—believing that even when we can't see the way forward, God's love is leading us. It's about trusting that there's a purpose to all of this, even if we don't understand it right now."

Grace nodded, her heart swelling with love for the man beside her. "Hope doesn't put us to shame, does it? That's what Romans 5:5 says—'And hope does not put us to shame, because God's love has been poured out into our hearts through the Holy Spirit, who has been given to us.' I think that's what we need to hold on to, Ethan. The hope that God's love is with us, guiding us, and that it won't let us down."

Ethan squeezed her hand, his eyes filled with warmth and affection. "I believe that, Grace. And I believe that as long as we hold on to that hope, we'll find our way through this uncertainty."

They sat together in comfortable silence, the weight of their conversation lifting as they allowed themselves to rest in the hope they had found. It wasn't a hope that promised an easy path, but it was a hope that promised they wouldn't walk that path alone. And for Grace and Ethan, that was enough.

As the weeks went by, Grace and Ethan continued to navigate the uncertainty of their future, but they did so with a renewed sense of hope and trust in God's plan. They began to take small steps toward their future, discussing their goals and dreams and making plans for the life they wanted to build together.

Ethan started exploring new opportunities in his career, considering options that would allow him to balance his work with his commitment to his relationship with Grace. It wasn't an easy process—there were moments of doubt and fear, times when the uncertainty seemed overwhelming—but he held on to the hope that God was leading him in the right direction.

Grace, too, began to find new ways to pursue her passions, taking on new projects and exploring opportunities that excited her. She found that as she let go of her need for control, she was able to embrace the uncertainty with a sense of curiosity and faith, trusting that God's love was guiding her.

Together, they learned to lean on each other, to support each other through the challenges they faced. They made time for the things that mattered most—prayer, communication, and quality time together—and they found that their relationship grew stronger as a result.

One evening, as they sat on the porch, watching the sun set over the city, Grace turned to Ethan with a thoughtful expression. "I've been thinking a lot about what we've been through lately," she began, her voice soft but filled with conviction. "And I've realized that the hope we've found, the trust we've placed in God's plan, has made us stronger. It's brought us closer together."

Ethan nodded, his gaze steady as he looked into her eyes. "I feel the same way, Grace. This journey hasn't been easy, but it's taught us to rely on each other and on God in ways we never have before. It's taught us that hope isn't just a feeling—it's a choice we make every day."

Grace smiled, her heart swelling with love and gratitude. "I'm so grateful for that, Ethan. I'm grateful that we've been able to hold on to hope, even when things were uncertain. And I'm grateful that we've been able to trust in God's love to guide us."

Ethan reached out and took her hand, his voice filled with emotion as he spoke. "I'm grateful too, Grace. I believe that as long as we continue to hold on to that hope, to trust in God's love, we'll be able to face whatever comes our way."

They sat together, their hands intertwined, the warmth of their connection filling the air around them. The uncertainty of their future hadn't disappeared, but it had been transformed into something else—something that felt more like possibility than fear. They knew that there would still be challenges ahead, but they also knew that they had the strength and the faith to face them together.

Theological Reflection

HOPE IS A CENTRAL THEME in the Christian faith, and it is deeply intertwined with love. In Romans 5:5, the Apostle Paul writes, "And hope does not put us to shame, because God's love has been poured out into our hearts through the Holy Spirit, who has been given to us." This verse reminds us that hope is not just a fleeting feeling—it is a steadfast trust in God's love, a belief that no matter what challenges we face, God's love will not let us down.

In the story of Grace and Ethan, we see the power of hope at work in their relationship. They faced uncertainty about their future, a fear that could have easily driven them apart. But instead of allowing that fear to take over, they chose to hold on to hope—to believe that God's love was guiding them, even when the path wasn't clear.

Hope in love is about more than just wishing for a better future—it is about trusting in the present moment, about believing that God is with us, guiding us through the challenges we face. It is about choosing to see the possibilities, even when the circumstances seem overwhelming. And it is about holding on to the belief that God's love is enough to carry us through, no matter what comes our way.

As we reflect on the relationship between love and hope, we are reminded that our ability to hope is rooted in the love we have received from God. Just as God's love has been poured out into our hearts, so too does that love give us the strength to hope, to trust, and to believe that there is a purpose to everything we go through.

May we always strive to hold on to hope in our relationships, to trust in God's love, and to believe that even in the midst of uncertainty, there is a plan and a purpose for our lives. And may we find the strength to choose hope, even when it is difficult, knowing that in doing so, we are reflecting the heart of God and experiencing the true power of love.

Chapter 10: Love's Truth

The air in the small apartment felt unusually heavy, as if the walls themselves were closing in. Grace Elliott sat on the edge of the bed, her hands clasped tightly in her lap, her heart pounding in her chest. The room was bathed in the soft light of the setting sun, but the warmth of the evening seemed to do little to ease the tension that hung between her and Ethan Matthews. This was a moment she had feared, yet also knew was inevitable—the moment when the truth had to be faced, no matter how painful it might be.

For weeks now, there had been a growing distance between them, a tension that neither had wanted to address directly. They had both felt it—the awkward silences, the forced smiles, the way their conversations had become more guarded, more careful. Something had shifted between them, and while they had both tried to ignore it, to pretend that everything was fine, the truth had become impossible to deny.

Grace's mind raced as she tried to find the right words, the right way to bring up what had been gnawing at her for so long. She loved Ethan deeply, but she couldn't shake the feeling that there was something he wasn't telling her, something that was slowly driving a wedge between them. And now, as they sat in the quiet of their home, the truth was the only thing that could either break them apart or set them free.

Ethan sat across from her, his expression tense and uncertain. He could feel the weight of her gaze, the unspoken questions that lingered in the air between them. He had been dreading this moment, the moment when he would have to come clean about what had been haunting him. The truth was something he had been running from, afraid of what it might mean for their relationship. But now, faced with the woman he loved, he knew that there was no more running. The truth had to come out, no matter the consequences.

Finally, unable to bear the silence any longer, Grace took a deep breath and spoke, her voice trembling with emotion. "Ethan, we need to talk about what's been going on between us. I can't keep pretending that everything is okay when it's not. I love you, but I need to know the truth. What's really been going on?"

Ethan looked up at her, his heart sinking at the pain in her voice. He had always prided himself on being honest, on building their relationship on a foundation of trust and openness. But now, he was faced with the reality that he had been keeping something from her, something that he knew could shatter the trust they had worked so hard to build.

"Grace," he began softly, his voice heavy with regret, "I haven't been completely honest with you. And I'm sorry for that. I've been struggling with something, and I've been too afraid to tell you because I didn't want to hurt you."

Grace's heart tightened in her chest as she listened to his words, a mixture of fear and relief washing over her. She had suspected that something was wrong, but hearing him admit it out loud made the situation all the more real. "What is it, Ethan? Please, just tell me the truth."

Ethan took a deep breath, his hands trembling slightly as he prepared to reveal what he had been hiding. "There's something that happened at work a few months ago... something I haven't told you about because I didn't want to worry you. I made a mistake, Grace. A big one."

Grace's breath caught in her throat as she listened, her mind racing with possibilities. "What kind of mistake?" she asked, her voice barely above a whisper.

Ethan looked down at his hands, unable to meet her eyes as he continued. "There was a patient I was treating... a young man who had come in with what seemed like a minor injury. I was in a rush that day, and I didn't take the time to fully assess his condition. I made a snap judgment, thinking it was just a sprain or something minor, and I sent him home with some painkillers."

He paused, his voice thick with emotion. "But it turned out that I was wrong. He had a serious internal injury that I didn't catch, and by the time he came back to the hospital, it was too late. He died, Grace. He died because of my mistake."

Grace felt her heart drop as she listened to his confession, her mind reeling with the weight of what he had just revealed. She had always known Ethan to be a dedicated and compassionate doctor, someone who took his responsibilities seriously. To hear that he had made such a grave error, and that he had been carrying the guilt of it for so long, was almost too much to bear.

"Oh, Ethan," she whispered, her voice filled with sorrow. "I'm so sorry. I can't imagine how hard this has been for you."

Ethan finally looked up at her, his eyes filled with tears. "I've been carrying this guilt with me for months, Grace. I've tried to move on, to keep doing my job, but it's been eating away at me. And I've been afraid to tell you because I didn't want you to see me differently. I didn't want to lose you."

Grace reached out and took his hand, her touch gentle and reassuring. "Ethan, you could never lose me. I love you, and nothing is going to change that. But I wish you had told me sooner. We're in this together, remember? You don't have to carry this burden alone."

Ethan's grip on her hand tightened as he nodded, his voice breaking with emotion. "I know, Grace. And I'm sorry for shutting you out, for not being honest with you. I was so afraid of what you would think of me, of what this might do to us."

Grace's heart ached as she looked at him, her love for him stronger than ever despite the pain of his confession. "Ethan, I'm not going to pretend that this isn't hard to hear. But what matters most to me is that you're being honest with me now. We can't build our relationship on lies or secrets. We need to be able to trust each other, even when the truth is difficult."

Ethan nodded, his eyes filled with gratitude and relief. "You're right, Grace. And I promise you, from now on, I'll always be honest with you. No more secrets, no more hiding. You deserve the truth, no matter how hard it is."

Grace felt a sense of peace wash over her as she listened to his words, the tension in her chest slowly beginning to ease. This was the moment of truth they had both been avoiding, but now that it was out in the open, she felt a renewed sense of hope for their relationship. It wouldn't be easy—there would be more difficult conversations, more challenges to face—but they had taken the first step toward healing and rebuilding the trust that had been shaken.

"Thank you for telling me the truth, Ethan," she said softly, her voice filled with love. "I know it wasn't easy, but I'm glad you did. We can get through this together, as long as we're honest with each other."

Ethan nodded, his heart swelling with love and gratitude for the woman beside him. "I love you, Grace. And I'm so grateful for your understanding, for your forgiveness. I promise I'll never take that for granted."

Grace smiled, her eyes misting over with tears as she looked at him. "I love you too, Ethan. And I'm committed to building our relationship on a foundation of truth and trust. That's the only way our love can truly grow."

They sat together in silence for a few moments, the weight of the conversation lifting as they allowed themselves to rest in the truth they had finally faced. The sun had dipped below the horizon, casting the room in a soft, dusky glow, but there was a sense of clarity between them now, a feeling that they had taken an important step toward healing and moving forward.

In the days that followed, Grace and Ethan continued to navigate the aftermath of their conversation, but they did so with a renewed sense of openness and honesty. They began to talk more freely about their fears, their hopes, and the challenges they were facing. The truth, which had once felt like a burden too heavy to bear, had become a source of strength, a reminder that their love could withstand even the most difficult of circumstances.

Ethan sought professional help to deal with the guilt and grief he had been carrying, and Grace supported him every step of the way. She knew that healing would take time, that there would be moments of doubt and struggle, but she also knew that they were on the right path—together.

One evening, as they sat on the couch, Ethan turned to Grace with a thoughtful expression. "I've been thinking a lot about what we talked about the other night," he began, his voice steady but serious. "About how important it is to be honest with each other, even when the truth is hard."

Grace nodded, her heart swelling with love for the man beside her. "I've been thinking about it too. I think that moment of truth was a turning point for us, Ethan. It was hard, but it brought us closer together."

Ethan reached out and took her hand, his eyes filled with warmth and affection. "It did. And it made me realize that love can't thrive in the darkness. It needs light—it needs truth. I don't ever want to go back to hiding things from you, Grace. I want us to build our relationship on a foundation of truth and trust, no matter what."

Grace smiled, her heart filled with gratitude and hope. "That's exactly what I want too, Ethan. I think that's what 1 Corinthians 13:6 is all about—'Love does not delight in evil but rejoices with the truth.' Our love can't grow if we're hiding things from each other. It can only grow when we're honest, even when it's difficult."

Ethan squeezed her hand, his voice filled with conviction. "You're right, Grace. And I'm committed to that—committed to being honest with you, to building our relationship on a foundation of truth. I know it won't always be easy, but I believe it's the only way we can truly move forward."

Grace felt a deep sense of peace wash over her as she listened to his words. She knew that their journey wasn't over, that there would still be challenges and difficult moments ahead. But she also knew that they were stronger now, that they had taken an important step toward building a relationship that was grounded in truth and trust.

"I'm committed to that too, Ethan," she said softly, her voice filled with love. "I want our love to be a reflection of God's love—a love that rejoices in the truth, that isn't afraid to face the difficult moments. I believe that's the kind of love that can last a lifetime."

Ethan smiled, his heart swelling with love and gratitude for the woman beside him. "I believe that too, Grace. And I'm so grateful to be on this journey with you."

They sat together in comfortable silence, the warmth of their connection filling the room. The truth had brought clarity to their relationship, a clarity that had been missing for too long. And with that clarity came a renewed sense of hope and commitment—a commitment to building a love that was strong, honest, and true.

Theological Reflection

TRUTH IS A CENTRAL theme in the Christian faith, and it is essential to any loving relationship. In 1 Corinthians 13:6, the Apostle Paul writes, "Love does not delight in evil but rejoices with the truth." This verse reminds us that true love cannot exist in the absence of truth. Love that is built on lies or deceit is fragile, easily shattered by the weight of dishonesty. But love that is grounded in truth is strong, enduring, and capable of withstanding even the most difficult challenges.

In the story of Grace and Ethan, we see the power of truth at work in their relationship. The moment of truth they faced was painful, a moment that could have driven them apart. But instead of allowing that truth to destroy their relationship, they chose to face it together, to be honest with each other, and to rebuild the trust that had been shaken.

Truth in love is about more than just being honest—it is about being open, vulnerable, and willing to face the difficult moments with courage and grace. It is about recognizing that love cannot thrive in the darkness, that it needs light and truth to grow. And it is about trusting that God's love is the ultimate source of truth, a love that rejoices in the light and guides us toward healing and wholeness.

As we reflect on the importance of truth in love, we are reminded that our ability to be truthful with others is rooted in the truth we have received from God. Just as God's love is honest, pure, and true, so too are we called to build our relationships on a foundation of truth and trust. It is through this truth that we are able to experience the fullness of love, to build relationships that are strong, healthy, and enduring.

May we always strive to be truthful in our relationships, to be open and honest with those we love, and to build our relationships on a foundation of truth and trust. And may we find the strength to rejoice in the truth, even when it is difficult, knowing that in doing so, we are reflecting the heart of God and experiencing the true power of love.

Chapter 11: Enduring Love

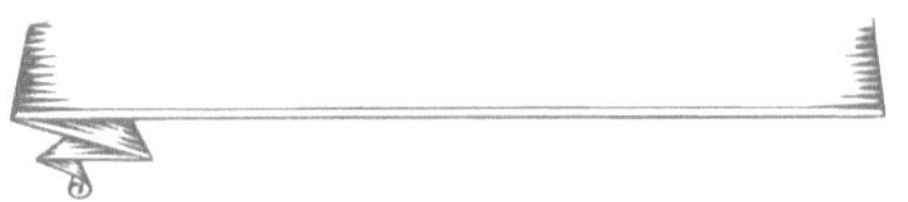

The cool breeze of an early autumn afternoon swept through the park, rustling the leaves that had just begun to turn vibrant shades of red, orange, and gold. The air was crisp, filled with the earthy scent of the changing season, and the sky above was a soft, pale blue, dotted with wispy clouds. It was a perfect day for a walk, the kind of day that made you feel alive, connected to the world around you. But for Grace Elliott and Ethan Matthews, this walk was about more than just enjoying the beauty of the season—it was about reconnecting with each other, reaffirming the commitment that had brought them together and carried them through so much.

They walked side by side along the path that wound through the park, their hands clasped together, their steps unhurried. The past year had been a challenging one for their relationship, filled with moments of doubt, fear, and uncertainty. They had faced trials that had tested the very foundation of their love, forcing them to confront truths they had long avoided, and to make choices that would shape the future of their relationship. But through it all, they had held on to each other, their love enduring despite the storms they had weathered.

As they walked, Grace glanced over at Ethan, her heart swelling with love and gratitude for the man beside her. She had always known that their love was something special, something worth fighting for, but it was only now, after everything they had been through, that she truly understood the depth of their connection. It was a love that had been tested, refined in the fire of adversity, and it had emerged stronger, more resilient than ever before.

Ethan felt Grace's gaze and turned to meet her eyes, a soft smile playing on his lips. He could see the love and warmth in her expression, and it filled him with a sense of peace and contentment. There had been times, not so long ago, when he had feared that their love might not survive the challenges they had faced. But now, as he walked beside her, he knew that their love had not only survived—it had flourished.

"Penny for your thoughts?" Ethan asked gently, squeezing Grace's hand as they walked.

Grace smiled, a soft blush coloring her cheeks. "I was just thinking about us," she replied, her voice filled with affection. "About everything we've been through, and how far we've come. I feel like we're stronger now than we've ever been."

Ethan nodded, his expression thoughtful. "I feel the same way. It hasn't been easy, but I think all the challenges we've faced have brought us closer together. We've learned so much about each other, about ourselves, and about what it really means to love someone."

Grace felt a warmth spread through her chest at his words, and she nodded in agreement. "It's true. I think we've learned that love isn't just about the good times—it's about standing by each other through the difficult times, too. It's about enduring, no matter what."

Ethan smiled, his eyes filled with admiration as he looked at her. "You know, that reminds me of something I've been thinking about a lot lately. It's from 1 Corinthians 13:7—'Love always protects, always trusts, always hopes, always perseveres.' I think that verse really captures what we've been trying to do, what we've been learning. Our love has endured because we've made a commitment to protect each other, to trust each other, to hold on to hope, and to persevere through whatever comes our way."

Grace's heart swelled with emotion as she listened to his words, the truth of them resonating deep within her. "I love that verse," she said softly, her voice trembling with emotion. "It's such a powerful reminder of what love is really all about. And I think it's something we can always come back to, no matter what challenges we face in the future."

Ethan nodded, his expression serious but filled with warmth. "I agree. And I want you to know, Grace, that I'm committed to this—to us. I'm committed to protecting our love, to trusting in it, to holding on to hope, and to persevering through whatever life throws at us. I know there will be more challenges ahead, but I believe that as long as we're in this together, we can get through anything."

Grace felt tears prick at the corners of her eyes as she looked at him, her heart overflowing with love and gratitude. "I'm committed to that too, Ethan. I know that our love can endure anything, as long as we keep choosing each other, keep choosing to love each other, every single day."

They walked in comfortable silence for a few moments, the sounds of the park—children playing, dogs barking, leaves rustling in the wind—filling the space between them. It was a peaceful, almost serene moment, one that felt like a calm after the storm. They had faced so much together, and now, as they walked side by side, they knew that they had emerged from those trials stronger, more united, more in love than ever before.

As they continued their walk, they came across a small, secluded bench nestled beneath a large oak tree. The bench was worn, the wood weathered by time and the elements, but it offered a perfect spot to sit and reflect. Ethan gestured toward the bench, and Grace nodded, a smile playing on her lips as they made their way over and sat down.

For a few moments, they simply sat in silence, enjoying the peace of the afternoon, the gentle rustling of the leaves above them, and the soft chirping of birds in the distance. It was a moment of quiet reflection, a time to simply be together, without the need for words.

Finally, Ethan broke the silence, his voice soft but filled with sincerity. "Grace, I want to ask you something," he began, his gaze steady as he looked into her eyes. "It's something I've been thinking about for a while now, and I think the time is right."

Grace felt her heart skip a beat at the seriousness in his tone, her breath catching in her throat as she waited for him to continue. "What is it, Ethan?" she asked softly, her voice barely above a whisper.

Ethan reached into his jacket pocket and pulled out a small, velvet box, holding it gently in his hand. Grace's eyes widened in surprise, her heart racing as she realized what was happening. "Ethan..." she began, her voice trembling with emotion.

Ethan smiled, his eyes filled with love as he opened the box to reveal a delicate, sparkling ring nestled inside. "Grace," he said, his voice steady but filled with emotion, "I've loved you from the moment I met you. You've been my partner, my confidante, my best friend, and the love of my life. We've been through so much together, and I can't imagine my life without you. I want to spend the rest of my life with you, facing whatever challenges come our way, building a life together that's grounded in love, trust, and faith. Grace, will you marry me?"

Tears filled Grace's eyes as she looked at the man she loved, her heart overflowing with joy and gratitude. She had dreamed of this moment for so long, but nothing could have prepared her for the overwhelming wave of emotion that washed over her now. "Yes, Ethan," she whispered, her voice thick with tears. "Yes, I'll marry you. I want to spend the rest of my life with you, too."

Ethan's smile widened, and he gently took the ring from the box, sliding it onto Grace's finger with a tenderness that made her heart ache with love. As soon as the ring was in place, Grace threw her arms around him, holding him close as tears of joy streamed down her face.

For a long moment, they simply held each other, the world around them fading away as they basked in the love they shared. It was a moment of pure, unadulterated joy, a moment that felt like the culmination of everything they had been through together, and the beginning of a new chapter in their lives.

Finally, Grace pulled back slightly, looking up at Ethan with a smile that lit up her entire face. "I love you so much, Ethan," she said softly, her voice filled with emotion. "I can't wait to start this new journey with you."

Ethan smiled, his heart swelling with love as he looked into her eyes. "I love you too, Grace. And I'm so excited to build our future together. I know that no matter what comes our way, we'll face it together, and our love will endure."

They spent the rest of the afternoon in the park, talking about their future, dreaming about the life they would build together. There was a sense of peace and contentment between them, a feeling that they were exactly where they were meant to be. They knew that there would still be challenges ahead, but they also knew that they had the strength and the love to face them together.

In the days and weeks that followed, Grace and Ethan began to make plans for their wedding, but more importantly, they began to make plans for their life together. They talked about their hopes and dreams, about the kind of marriage they wanted to build, and the kind of love they wanted to share.

They knew that marriage was not just about the big moments—the wedding, the honeymoon, the celebrations—but about the everyday moments, the small acts of love and kindness that would sustain them through the years. They made a commitment to each other, to always protect their love, to always trust in each other, to always hold on to hope, and to always persevere, no matter what challenges came their way.

One evening, as they sat together on the couch, Grace turned to Ethan with a thoughtful expression. "I've been thinking a lot about what it means to build a marriage that lasts," she began, her voice soft but filled with conviction. "I think it's about more than just loving each other—it's about making a choice, every day, to protect our love, to trust in it, to hold on to hope, and to persevere through whatever comes our way."

Ethan nodded, his gaze steady as he looked into her eyes. "I think you're right, Grace. Love isn't just a feeling—it's a choice. It's a commitment to stand by each other, to support each other, to lift each other up, even when things get tough. And I believe that as long as we keep making that choice, our love will endure."

Grace smiled, her heart swelling with love and gratitude for the man beside her. "I believe that too, Ethan. And I'm so grateful that we're in this together."

They spent the rest of the evening talking about their future, about the life they wanted to build together. There was a sense of excitement and anticipation between them, a feeling that they were on the brink of something truly special. They knew that their love had already endured so much, and they were confident that it would continue to endure, no matter what challenges came their way.

As the months passed, Grace and Ethan continued to build their life together, always keeping in mind the commitment they had made to each other. They celebrated the small moments, the everyday victories, and they supported each other through the challenges and setbacks that inevitably came their way.

One evening, as they sat together in their living room, the soft glow of the fire casting a warm light across the room, Grace turned to Ethan with a thoughtful expression. "I've been thinking a lot about the future," she began, her voice soft but filled with conviction. "About what it means to build a marriage that lasts, to build a love that endures."

Ethan nodded, his gaze steady as he looked into her eyes. "I've been thinking about that too, Grace. I think it's about more than just loving each other—it's about making a choice, every day, to protect our love, to trust in it, to hold on to hope, and to persevere through whatever comes our way."

Grace smiled, her heart swelling with love and gratitude for the man beside her. "I think you're right, Ethan. And I'm so grateful that we're in this together."

They spent the rest of the evening talking about their future, about the life they wanted to build together. There was a sense of excitement and anticipation between them, a feeling that they were on the brink of something truly special. They knew that their love had already endured so much, and they were confident that it would continue to endure, no matter what challenges came their way.

As the years passed, Grace and Ethan's love continued to grow and deepen. They faced challenges and setbacks, but they always faced them together, always holding on to the commitment they had made to each other. Their love was not perfect—there were moments of frustration, moments of doubt—but it was a love that endured, a love that was built on a foundation of trust, hope, and perseverance.

One evening, as they sat together on the porch, watching the sun set over the city, Grace turned to Ethan with a smile. "I've been thinking a lot about our journey," she began, her voice soft but filled with emotion. "About everything we've been through, and how far we've come. I feel like our love has only grown stronger over the years."

Ethan nodded, his expression thoughtful. "I feel the same way, Grace. It hasn't always been easy, but I think that's what makes our love so special. It's a love that has endured, a love that has been tested and has come out stronger on the other side."

Grace smiled, her heart swelling with love and gratitude for the man beside her. "I'm so grateful for that, Ethan. I'm so grateful for you, for the life we've built together."

Ethan reached out and took her hand, his voice filled with warmth and affection. "I'm grateful too, Grace. And I believe that as long as we continue to make the choice to love each other, to protect our love, to trust in it, to hold on to hope, and to persevere, our love will continue to endure."

They sat together in comfortable silence, the warmth of their connection filling the air around them. The sun had dipped below the horizon, casting the sky in shades of pink and purple, and there was a sense of peace and contentment between them, a feeling that they had found something truly special in each other.

They knew that their journey was far from over, that there would still be challenges and difficult moments ahead. But they also knew that they had the strength and the love to face them together. Their love had endured so much already, and they were confident that it would continue to endure, no matter what came their way.

Theological Reflection

ENDURANCE IS A CENTRAL theme in the Christian faith, and it is essential to any loving relationship. In 1 Corinthians 13:7, the Apostle Paul writes, "Love always protects, always trusts, always hopes, always perseveres." This verse reminds us that true love is not just about the good times—it is about standing by each other through the difficult times, about making a commitment to protect, trust, hope, and persevere, no matter what challenges come our way.

In the story of Grace and Ethan, we see the power of enduring love at work in their relationship. They faced challenges and setbacks, moments of doubt and fear, but they always held on to the commitment they had made to each other. Their love endured because they made a choice—every day—to protect their love, to trust in it, to hold on to hope, and to persevere through whatever came their way.

Enduring love is about more than just feelings—it is about making a choice, every day, to love each other, to support each other, to lift each other up, even when things get tough. It is about trusting that God's love is the ultimate source of endurance, a love that protects, trusts, hopes, and perseveres through all circumstances.

As we reflect on the endurance of love, we are reminded that our ability to endure in love is rooted in the love we have received from God. Just as God's love is steadfast, unchanging, and enduring, so too are we called to build our relationships on a foundation of trust, hope, and perseverance. It is through this endurance that we are able to experience the fullness of love, to build relationships that are strong, healthy, and enduring.

May we always strive to protect, trust, hope, and persevere in our relationships, to make the choice to love each other every day, and to build our relationships on a foundation of enduring love. And may we find the strength to endure, even when it is difficult, knowing that in doing so, we are reflecting the heart of God and experiencing the true power of love.

Chapter 12: The Power of Love

The first light of dawn was just beginning to peek over the horizon, casting a soft, golden glow across the quiet neighborhood. The world was still, the usual sounds of city life hushed in the early morning calm. Inside their cozy apartment, Grace Elliott lay in bed, her head resting on Ethan Matthews' chest, listening to the steady rhythm of his heartbeat. It was a sound she had come to cherish, a sound that brought her comfort and peace, reminding her that she was safe, that she was loved.

For so long, she had dreamed of finding a love like this—a love that was deep, abiding, and transformative. But now that she had it, she realized that it was so much more than she had ever imagined. It wasn't just the warmth and joy she felt when she was with Ethan, or the way he made her feel valued and cherished. It was the way their love had changed her, had transformed her from the inside out. It was the way it had healed old wounds, driven out old fears, and made her into the person she had always wanted to be.

She shifted slightly, lifting her head to look up at Ethan. His face was relaxed in sleep, his features softened in the pale light of morning. Even now, after everything they had been through, she was still struck by how deeply she loved him, how much he had come to mean to her. But it wasn't just the man he was—it was the way he had helped her become the woman she was now, the way their love had brought out the best in her, had helped her grow and heal in ways she never thought possible.

As she lay there, watching the sunlight slowly fill the room, her mind drifted back over the past few years, to the moments that had brought them to this place, to the journey they had been on together. There had been times when she had doubted, times when she had been afraid, times when she had wondered if their love was strong enough to withstand the trials they faced. But through it all, they had held on to each other, had clung to the love that had brought them together, and that love had seen them through.

It was a love that had transformed her, had taken the broken pieces of her heart and made them whole again. It was a love that had driven out the fear that had once held her captive, had replaced it with a sense of peace and security she had never known before. And now, as she lay beside the man she loved, she realized that this love had not only changed her—it had changed them both.

Ethan stirred beside her, his eyes fluttering open as he slowly awoke. A smile spread across his face as he saw her lying there, watching him, and he reached up to gently brush a strand of hair behind her ear. "Good morning," he murmured, his voice husky with sleep.

"Good morning," Grace replied, her voice soft and filled with affection. She leaned down to press a kiss to his lips, savoring the warmth and tenderness of the moment. "Did you sleep well?"

Ethan nodded, his hand moving to rest on her back as he pulled her closer. "I always sleep well when I'm with you," he said with a smile, his eyes filled with love.

Grace felt her heart swell at his words, a sense of deep contentment settling over her. "I was just thinking," she began, her voice thoughtful, "about how much our love has changed me. How it's healed me, made me into a better person."

Ethan's expression softened as he looked at her, his eyes filled with warmth and understanding. "I feel the same way, Grace. Loving you has changed me too. It's made me stronger, more compassionate, more open. I never realized how much love could transform a person until I met you."

Grace's eyes filled with tears as she listened to his words, her heart overflowing with emotion. "It's amazing, isn't it? How love can take something broken and make it whole again? How it can drive out fear and replace it with something so much stronger?"

Ethan nodded, his gaze steady as he looked into her eyes. "It is. I think that's what makes love so powerful—it's not just about the feelings we have for each other, it's about how those feelings change us, how they help us grow and become the best versions of ourselves. It's about the way love heals old wounds, the way it gives us the strength to face our fears and overcome them."

Grace felt a tear slip down her cheek as she listened to his words, her heart aching with love for the man beside her. "You've done that for me, Ethan," she said softly, her voice trembling with emotion. "You've helped me heal in ways I never thought possible. You've driven out the fear that used to control me, and you've made me feel safe, loved, and cherished. I can't thank you enough for that."

Ethan's eyes filled with tears as he reached up to cup her face in his hands, his voice thick with emotion as he spoke. "And you've done the same for me, Grace. You've helped me see the world in a different way, helped me find strength and courage I didn't know I had. You've shown me what it means to truly love someone, and I can't imagine my life without you."

They held each other for a long moment, the weight of their words hanging in the air between them. It was a moment of pure, unfiltered love—a love that had been tested, had been refined in the fire of adversity, and had emerged stronger and more powerful than ever before.

Finally, Grace pulled back slightly, her eyes filled with determination as she looked into Ethan's eyes. "I want us to keep growing together, Ethan," she said softly, her voice filled with conviction. "I want us to keep learning from each other, to keep healing each other, to keep driving out the fear and replacing it with love. I want us to keep becoming the best versions of ourselves, together."

Ethan smiled, his heart swelling with love and admiration for the woman beside him. "I want that too, Grace. I want us to keep building a life together that's grounded in love, trust, and faith. I want us to keep showing each other the power of love, every single day."

Grace felt a deep sense of peace settle over her as she listened to his words, the warmth of his love filling her heart. "We will, Ethan. We'll keep growing, keep healing, keep loving. And we'll do it together."

AS THE DAYS TURNED into weeks, Grace and Ethan continued to explore the transformative power of love in their lives. They talked openly about the ways their love had changed them, the ways it had healed old wounds and driven out old fears. They reflected on the journey they had been on together, the challenges they had faced, and the ways those challenges had brought them closer, had strengthened their bond and deepened their love.

One evening, as they sat together on the porch, watching the sun set over the city, Grace turned to Ethan with a thoughtful expression. "I've been thinking a lot about how much we've grown together," she began, her voice soft but filled with conviction. "About how much our love has changed us, made us into better people."

Ethan nodded, his gaze steady as he looked into her eyes. "I've been thinking about that too, Grace. I think it's one of the most amazing things about love—how it can take something broken and make it whole again, how it can drive out fear and replace it with something so much stronger."

Grace smiled, her heart swelling with love and gratitude. "I think that's what 1 John 4:18 is all about—'There is no fear in love. But perfect love drives out fear...' Our love has driven out so much fear in my life, Ethan. It's given me a sense of peace and security I never knew before. And I'm so grateful for that."

Ethan reached out and took her hand, his voice filled with warmth and affection. "I'm grateful for that too, Grace. Our love has given me a strength I didn't know I had, a courage to face my fears and overcome them. And I believe that as long as we keep loving each other, as long as we keep showing each other the power of love, we'll continue to grow and heal together."

Grace felt tears prick at the corners of her eyes as she listened to his words, her heart overflowing with emotion. "I believe that too, Ethan. I believe that our love has the power to change us, to heal us, to make us into the best versions of ourselves. And I want us to keep growing together, to keep loving each other in a way that drives out fear and replaces it with something so much stronger."

Ethan smiled, his eyes filled with love and admiration for the woman beside him. "We will, Grace. We'll keep growing, keep healing, keep loving. And we'll do it together, every step of the way."

They sat together in comfortable silence, the warmth of their connection filling the air around them. The sun had dipped below the horizon, casting the sky in shades of pink and purple, and there was a sense of peace and contentment between them, a feeling that they were exactly where they were meant to be.

In the months that followed, Grace and Ethan continued to explore the power of love in their lives, always striving to grow and heal together. They made a conscious effort to show each other love in the small, everyday moments—to be patient, to be kind, to be understanding and compassionate. They knew that love wasn't just about the big, dramatic gestures, but about the quiet, consistent acts of care and consideration that made up the fabric of their relationship.

One evening, as they sat together on the couch, Grace turned to Ethan with a thoughtful expression. "I've been thinking a lot about what it means to love someone," she began, her voice soft but filled with conviction. "About how love isn't just about how we feel—it's about what we do, about the choices we make every day to show each other that we care, that we're committed to each other."

Ethan nodded, his gaze steady as he looked into her eyes. "I think you're right, Grace. Love is a choice—it's a commitment to stand by each other, to support each other, to lift each other up, even when things get tough. It's about choosing to love each other, every single day, in the big moments and the small ones."

Grace smiled, her heart swelling with love and gratitude for the man beside her. "I think that's what makes love so powerful—it's not just about the feelings we have, but about the actions we take, the choices we make to show each other that we care. It's about the way we choose to love each other, even when it's difficult, even when we're tired or frustrated. That's the kind of love that changes us, that heals us, that makes us into the best versions of ourselves."

Ethan reached out and took her hand, his voice filled with warmth and affection. "I think you're right, Grace. And I'm so grateful that we're in this together, that we're committed to loving each other in a way that's powerful, that's transformative. I believe that as long as we keep making that choice, our love will continue to change us, to heal us, to make us stronger."

Grace felt tears prick at the corners of her eyes as she listened to his words, her heart overflowing with emotion. "I'm so grateful for that too, Ethan. I'm so grateful for you, for the love we share. And I'm committed to continuing to grow and heal together, to continuing to show each other the power of love, every single day."

They spent the rest of the evening talking about their future, about the life they wanted to build together. There was a sense of excitement and anticipation between them, a feeling that they were on the brink of something truly special. They knew that their love had already changed them in so many ways, and they were confident that it would continue to do so, no matter what challenges came their way.

As the years passed, Grace and Ethan's love continued to grow and deepen. They faced challenges and setbacks, moments of doubt and fear, but they always faced them together, always holding on to the love that had brought them together. Their love was not perfect—there were moments of frustration, moments of disagreement—but it was a love that had the power to change, to heal, to make them into the best versions of themselves.

One evening, as they sat together on the porch, watching the sun set over the city, Grace turned to Ethan with a smile. "I've been thinking a lot about our journey," she began, her voice soft but filled with emotion. "About everything we've been through, and how much we've changed, how much we've grown together."

Ethan nodded, his expression thoughtful. "I've been thinking about that too, Grace. I think that's one of the most amazing things about love—how it has the power to change us, to heal us, to make us into the best versions of ourselves. I've seen that in you, in us, and I'm so grateful for it."

Grace smiled, her heart swelling with love and gratitude for the man beside her. "I'm so grateful for that too, Ethan. I'm so grateful for you, for the love we share. I believe that our love has the power to continue to change us, to continue to heal us, to make us stronger, no matter what comes our way."

Ethan reached out and took her hand, his voice filled with warmth and affection. "I believe that too, Grace. And I'm committed to continuing to show you the power of love, every single day. I know that as long as we keep making that choice, our love will continue to grow, to heal, to transform us."

They sat together in comfortable silence, the warmth of their connection filling the air around them. The sun had dipped below the horizon, casting the sky in shades of pink and purple, and there was a sense of peace and contentment between them, a feeling that they had found something truly special in each other.

They knew that their journey was far from over, that there would still be challenges and difficult moments ahead. But they also knew that they had the strength and the love to face them together. Their love had already changed them in so many ways, and they were confident that it would continue to do so, no matter what came their way.

Theological Reflection

LOVE HAS A TRANSFORMATIVE power that is central to the Christian faith. In 1 John 4:18, the Apostle John writes, "There is no fear in love. But perfect love drives out fear..." This verse reminds us that love is not just an emotion—it is a force that has the power to change us, to heal us, to drive out the fear that once held us captive.

In the story of Grace and Ethan, we see the power of love at work in their lives. Their love has not only brought them together—it has transformed them, has made them into better, stronger, more compassionate people. It has driven out the fear that once held them back, and it has replaced that fear with a sense of peace, security, and hope.

The power of love is not just about the feelings we have—it is about the actions we take, the choices we make every day to show each other that we care, that we are committed to each other. It is about the way love changes us, heals us, makes us into the best versions of ourselves. It is about the way love drives out fear and replaces it with something so much stronger.

As we reflect on the power of love, we are reminded that our ability to love is rooted in the love we have received from God. Just as God's love is perfect, unchanging, and transformative, so too are we called to love each other in a way that drives out fear, that heals old wounds, that makes us into the best versions of ourselves. It is through this love that we are able to experience the fullness of life, to build relationships that are strong, healthy, and enduring.

May we always strive to love each other in a way that is powerful, that is transformative, that drives out fear and replaces it with peace and security. And may we find the strength to continue to grow, to continue to heal, to continue to love each other in a way that reflects the heart of God and the true power of love.

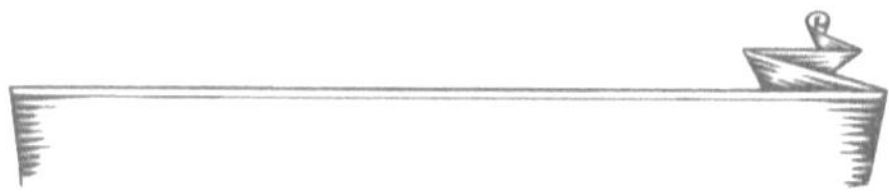

Chapter 13: Love's Promise Fulfilled

The morning sun streamed through the large windows of the cozy home that Grace Elliott and Ethan Matthews had built together, casting a warm, golden light across the room. The scent of freshly brewed coffee filled the air, mingling with the soft sounds of birds chirping outside. It was a peaceful morning, one of those rare moments when the world seemed to slow down, allowing them to simply be together, to savor the life they had created.

Grace sat at the kitchen table, her hands wrapped around a steaming mug of coffee, her eyes drifting over the familiar details of their home. The framed photos on the walls, the bookshelves filled with their favorite novels, the comfortable furniture that invited them to relax and unwind—every inch of this space was a testament to the love they had shared, the life they had built together over the years.

She had always dreamed of having a home like this, a place filled with warmth, love, and joy. But it was more than just the physical space that made this home special—it was the promise that had brought them together, the promise that had been fulfilled in ways she could never have imagined.

Grace's thoughts were interrupted by the sound of soft footsteps approaching from the hallway. She looked up to see Ethan entering the kitchen, his hair slightly tousled from sleep, a warm smile on his face as he approached her. He leaned down to press a kiss to her forehead, his touch gentle and familiar, and then took the seat across from her.

"Good morning," Ethan said, his voice filled with affection as he reached for his own mug of coffee. "How did you sleep?"

Grace smiled, her heart swelling with love for the man beside her. "I slept well," she replied softly, her eyes filled with warmth. "It was one of those nights where everything just felt right, you know?"

Ethan nodded, his gaze steady as he looked into her eyes. "I know exactly what you mean. It's mornings like this that make me realize how blessed we are, how much we've been given."

Grace's smile widened, and she reached across the table to take his hand in hers. "I was just thinking the same thing. I can't believe how far we've come, how much our love has grown and flourished. It feels like we're living in the fulfillment of the promise that brought us together."

Ethan squeezed her hand gently, his eyes filled with love and gratitude. "We are, Grace. We've seen the fruits of our love in so many ways—in our home, in our relationship, in the way we've supported each other through everything. I feel like we're living proof of God's promises."

Grace felt tears prick at the corners of her eyes as she listened to his words, her heart overflowing with emotion. "It's amazing, isn't it? How God's promises have been fulfilled in our lives? I never could have imagined all of this when we first started out, but now, looking back, I can see how every step of our journey has led us to this moment."

Ethan's smile was soft, filled with the quiet wisdom that had come from years of walking this path together. "God's promises are always greater than anything we could imagine. I think that's what makes them so precious, so powerful. They're not just about the blessings we receive—they're about the way those blessings transform us, the way they shape our lives and our love."

Grace nodded, her heart swelling with gratitude. "You're right, Ethan. And I'm so grateful that we've been able to experience that together, that we've been able to see the fulfillment of God's promises in our love."

They sat in comfortable silence for a few moments, the warmth of their connection filling the air around them. The morning light continued to stream through the windows, casting a golden glow over the room, and for a moment, it felt as if time itself had paused, allowing them to simply bask in the love they shared.

Finally, Ethan broke the silence, his voice filled with a quiet, thoughtful tone. "I've been thinking a lot about the promises we made to each other when we first started this journey," he said softly, his eyes meeting Grace's. "About how we promised to love each other, to support each other, to build a life together that was grounded in faith and trust."

Grace smiled, her heart swelling with love as she listened to his words. "I remember those promises, Ethan. And I think we've done a pretty good job of keeping them, don't you?"

Ethan's smile widened, his eyes twinkling with affection. "I think we have. But it's not just about the promises we made to each other—it's about the promises God made to us, the promises that have been fulfilled in our lives. I think about 2 Peter 1:4, where it says, 'Through these he has given us his very great and precious promises...' I feel like that verse really speaks to what we've experienced, to the way God's promises have been fulfilled in our love."

Grace felt a tear slip down her cheek as she listened to his words, her heart overflowing with gratitude. "It does, Ethan. God's promises have been so precious to us, haven't they? They've guided us, sustained us, and brought us to this place of fulfillment. I'm so grateful for that, for the way God's love has been made manifest in our lives."

Ethan nodded, his gaze steady as he looked into her eyes. "I'm grateful too, Grace. And I believe that as long as we continue to trust in God's promises, as long as we continue to walk this path together, we'll continue to see the fruits of that love in our lives."

Grace smiled, her heart filled with love and gratitude. "I believe that too, Ethan. And I'm so excited to see what the future holds for us, to see how God's promises will continue to be fulfilled in our love."

They sat together in comfortable silence, the warmth of their connection filling the air around them. The sun had risen higher in the sky, casting a bright, golden light across the room, and there was a sense of peace and contentment between them, a feeling that they were exactly where they were meant to be.

As the weeks and months passed, Grace and Ethan continued to experience the fulfillment of the promises that had brought them together. They saw the fruits of their love in the way they supported each other, in the way they nurtured their relationship, and in the way they built a life that was grounded in faith and trust.

One day, as they sat together in their living room, Grace turned to Ethan with a thoughtful expression. "I've been thinking a lot about the promises we made to each other when we first started this journey," she began, her voice soft but filled with conviction. "About how we promised to love each other, to support each other, to build a life together that was grounded in faith and trust."

Ethan nodded, his gaze steady as he looked into her eyes. "I've been thinking about that too, Grace. And I think we've done a pretty good job of keeping those promises, don't you?"

Grace smiled, her heart swelling with love and gratitude. "I think we have. But it's not just about the promises we made to each other—it's about the promises God made to us, the promises that have been fulfilled in our lives. I think about 2 Peter 1:4, where it says, 'Through these he has given us his very great and precious promises...' I feel like that verse really speaks to what we've experienced, to the way God's promises have been fulfilled in our love."

Ethan's smile widened, his eyes twinkling with affection. "It does, Grace. God's promises have been so precious to us, haven't they? They've guided us, sustained us, and brought us to this place of fulfillment. I'm so grateful for that, for the way God's love has been made manifest in our lives."

Grace felt a tear slip down her cheek as she listened to his words, her heart overflowing with gratitude. "I'm so grateful for that too, Ethan. I'm so grateful for the love we share, for the life we've built together. And I believe that as long as we continue to trust in God's promises, as long as we continue to walk this path together, we'll continue to see the fruits of that love in our lives."

Ethan nodded, his gaze steady as he looked into her eyes. "I believe that too, Grace. And I'm so excited to see what the future holds for us, to see how God's promises will continue to be fulfilled in our love."

They sat together in comfortable silence, the warmth of their connection filling the air around them. The sun had risen higher in the sky, casting a bright, golden light across the room, and there was a sense of peace and contentment between them, a feeling that they were exactly where they were meant to be.

As the years passed, Grace and Ethan continued to see the fulfillment of God's promises in their lives. They faced challenges and setbacks, moments of doubt and fear, but they always faced them together, always holding on to the love that had brought them together. Their love was not perfect—there were moments of frustration, moments of disagreement—but it was a love that had the power to change, to heal, to make them into the best versions of themselves.

One evening, as they sat together on the porch, watching the sun set over the city, Grace turned to Ethan with a smile. "I've been thinking a lot about our journey," she began, her voice soft but filled with emotion. "About everything we've been through, and how much we've changed, how much we've grown together."

Ethan nodded, his expression thoughtful. "I've been thinking about that too, Grace. I think that's one of the most amazing things about love—how it has the power to change us, to heal us, to make us into the best versions of ourselves. I've seen that in you, in us, and I'm so grateful for it."

Grace smiled, her heart swelling with love and gratitude for the man beside her. "I'm so grateful for that too, Ethan. I'm so grateful for you, for the love we share. I believe that our love has the power to continue to change us, to continue to heal us, to make us stronger, no matter what comes our way."

Ethan reached out and took her hand, his voice filled with warmth and affection. "I believe that too, Grace. And I'm committed to continuing to show you the power of love, every single day. I know that as long as we keep making that choice, our love will continue to grow, to heal, to transform us."

They sat together in comfortable silence, the warmth of their connection filling the air around them. The sun had dipped below the horizon, casting the sky in shades of pink and purple, and there was a sense of peace and contentment between them, a feeling that they had found something truly special in each other.

They knew that their journey was far from over, that there would still be challenges and difficult moments ahead. But they also knew that they had the strength and the love to face them together. Their love had already changed them in so many ways, and they were confident that it would continue to do so, no matter what came their way.

Theological Reflection

THE FULFILLMENT OF God's promises is a central theme in the Christian faith, and it is deeply intertwined with love. In 2 Peter 1:4, the Apostle Peter writes, "Through these he has given us his very great and precious promises..." This verse reminds us that God's promises are not just about the blessings we receive—they are about the way those blessings transform us, the way they shape our lives and our love.

In the story of Grace and Ethan, we see the fulfillment of God's promises in their lives. Their love has not only brought them together—it has transformed them, has made them into better, stronger, more compassionate people. It has driven out the fear that once held them back, and it has replaced that fear with a sense of peace, security, and hope.

The fulfillment of God's promises is not just about the end result—it is about the journey, the way those promises are fulfilled in our lives over time. It is about the way God's love guides us, sustains us, and brings us to a place of fulfillment. And it is about the way those promises change us, make us into the best versions of ourselves, and bring us closer to God and to each other.

As we reflect on the fulfillment of God's promises in love, we are reminded that our ability to experience those promises is rooted in the love we have received from God. Just as God's love is perfect, unchanging, and transformative, so too are we called to love each other in a way that reflects that love, that trusts in God's promises, and that experiences the fulfillment of those promises in our lives.

May we always strive to love each other in a way that is powerful, that is transformative, that drives out fear and replaces it with peace and security. And may we find the strength to continue to grow, to continue to heal, to continue to love each other in a way that reflects the heart of God and the true power of love.

Chapter 14: Love's Eternal Nature

The night sky was clear, a deep, velvety blue scattered with countless stars that shimmered like diamonds. A gentle breeze rustled the leaves of the old oak tree in the backyard, carrying with it the scent of blooming jasmine and freshly cut grass. The world seemed to be at peace, bathed in the soft glow of the moonlight that illuminated the landscape with a quiet serenity.

Grace Elliott and Ethan Matthews sat together on a weathered wooden bench beneath the oak tree, their hands intertwined, their gazes turned upward toward the heavens. It was one of those rare moments when time seemed to stand still, when the worries and concerns of everyday life faded away, leaving only the profound sense of connection between them.

They had shared countless moments like this over the years, moments of quiet reflection, of deep conversation, of simply being together. But tonight felt different. There was a sense of finality in the air, a feeling that they had reached a turning point in their journey, a point where they could look back and see how far they had come, and look forward with a sense of peace and assurance about the future.

For a long time, they sat in comfortable silence, listening to the sounds of the night—the distant chirping of crickets, the rustling of leaves in the breeze, the occasional hoot of an owl hidden in the branches above. It was a silence filled with meaning, a silence that spoke of the love they shared, a love that had grown and deepened over the years, a love that had weathered storms and emerged stronger on the other side.

Finally, Ethan broke the silence, his voice soft and thoughtful as he spoke. "It's nights like this that make me think about the bigger picture," he began, his gaze still fixed on the stars above. "About how our love is part of something so much greater, something eternal."

Grace turned to look at him, her heart swelling with love and admiration for the man beside her. "I've been thinking about that too," she replied, her voice filled with emotion. "About how our love connects us, not just to each other, but to something far beyond ourselves. It's like our love is a reflection of God's love, a small piece of something infinite and eternal."

Ethan nodded, his expression serious but filled with warmth. "Exactly. It's like what 1 Corinthians 13:8 says—'Love never fails. But where there are prophecies, they will cease; where there are tongues, they will be stilled; where there is knowledge, it will pass away.' Everything else in this world is temporary, but love... love is eternal. It never fails, it never ends."

Grace felt tears prick at the corners of her eyes as she listened to his words, the truth of them resonating deep within her. "That's such a comforting thought, isn't it? That no matter what happens, no matter what challenges we face, our love will endure. It's not just about this life—it's about something that goes beyond time, something that connects us to God and to each other for eternity."

Ethan squeezed her hand gently, his gaze steady as he looked into her eyes. "It is comforting. And it gives me so much peace to know that our love isn't just for this lifetime—it's something that will last forever, something that's part of God's eternal plan."

Grace smiled, her heart overflowing with love and gratitude. "I feel the same way, Ethan. I feel like our love has given me a glimpse of something so much greater, something eternal. It's like our love is a way for us to experience a little piece of heaven here on earth."

Ethan's smile widened, his eyes twinkling with affection. "I couldn't have said it better myself. Our love is a gift, a blessing, and it's something that will continue to grow and flourish, not just in this life, but for all eternity."

They sat together in silence for a few moments, the weight of their conversation settling over them like a warm blanket. The stars above continued to shimmer and dance in the night sky, a reminder of the vastness of the universe, and of the eternal nature of the love they shared.

Finally, Grace spoke again, her voice filled with quiet conviction. "I've always believed that love is the most powerful force in the world," she began, her gaze still fixed on the stars above. "It's the one thing that can overcome anything, that can heal any wound, that can bring people together in a way that nothing else can. And now, after everything we've been through, I believe that even more."

Ethan nodded, his expression thoughtful. "Love is powerful. It's what has carried us through the toughest times, what has brought us closer together, what has made us stronger. And it's what will continue to sustain us, no matter what the future holds."

Grace turned to look at him, her eyes filled with love and gratitude. "Our love is a reflection of God's love," she said softly, her voice trembling with emotion. "It's a reminder that we are never alone, that we are connected to something far greater than ourselves. It's a promise that no matter what happens, our love will endure, because it's part of something eternal."

Ethan smiled, his heart swelling with love for the woman beside him. "It's a promise I'm so grateful for, Grace. And it's a promise I intend to keep, every single day, for the rest of my life—and beyond."

Grace felt tears slip down her cheeks as she listened to his words, her heart overflowing with emotion. "I'm so grateful for that too, Ethan. I'm so grateful for you, for the love we share. And I believe that our love will continue to grow, to deepen, to become even more beautiful, because it's part of something eternal."

They sat together in silence once more, their hands intertwined, their hearts connected in a way that went beyond words. The night was still, the world around them quiet and peaceful, and for a moment, it felt as if they were the only two people in the universe, their love shining as brightly as the stars above.

As the days turned into weeks, and the weeks into months, Grace and Ethan continued to explore the eternal nature of the love they shared. They talked often about the ways their love had grown and deepened, about the ways it had connected them to each other and to God. They reflected on the journey they had been on together, the challenges they had faced, and the ways those challenges had strengthened their bond and made their love even more enduring.

One evening, as they sat together on the porch, watching the sun set over the city, Grace turned to Ethan with a thoughtful expression. "I've been thinking a lot about what it means to love someone eternally," she began, her voice soft but filled with conviction. "About how our love isn't just for this lifetime—it's something that will last forever, something that will continue to grow and flourish, even after we're gone."

Ethan nodded, his gaze steady as he looked into her eyes. "I've been thinking about that too, Grace. And I think that's one of the most amazing things about love—how it has the power to transcend time, to connect us to something far greater than ourselves. It's like our love is a reflection of God's love, a small piece of something infinite and eternal."

Grace smiled, her heart swelling with love and gratitude. "It's such a comforting thought, isn't it? That no matter what happens, no matter what challenges we face, our love will endure. It's not just about this life—it's about something that goes beyond time, something that connects us to God and to each other for eternity."

Ethan's smile widened, his eyes twinkling with affection. "It is comforting. And it gives me so much peace to know that our love isn't just for this lifetime—it's something that will last forever, something that's part of God's eternal plan."

They sat together in comfortable silence, the warmth of their connection filling the air around them. The sun had dipped below the horizon, casting the sky in shades of pink and purple, and there was a sense of peace and contentment between them, a feeling that they were exactly where they were meant to be.

In the years that followed, Grace and Ethan continued to experience the eternal nature of the love they shared. They faced challenges and setbacks, moments of doubt and fear, but they always faced them together, always holding on to the love that had brought them together. Their love was not perfect—there were moments of frustration, moments of disagreement—but it was a love that had the power to change, to heal, to make them into the best versions of themselves.

One evening, as they sat together on the porch, watching the sun set over the city, Grace turned to Ethan with a smile. "I've been thinking a lot about our journey," she began, her voice soft but filled with emotion. "About everything we've been through, and how much we've changed, how much we've grown together."

Ethan nodded, his expression thoughtful. "I've been thinking about that too, Grace. I think that's one of the most amazing things about love—how it has the power to change us, to heal us, to make us into the best versions of ourselves. I've seen that in you, in us, and I'm so grateful for it."

Grace smiled, her heart swelling with love and gratitude for the man beside her. "I'm so grateful for that too, Ethan. I'm so grateful for you, for the love we share. I believe that our love has the power to continue to change us, to continue to heal us, to make us stronger, no matter what comes our way."

Ethan reached out and took her hand, his voice filled with warmth and affection. "I believe that too, Grace. And I'm committed to continuing to show you the power of love, every single day. I know that as long as we keep making that choice, our love will continue to grow, to heal, to transform us."

They sat together in comfortable silence, the warmth of their connection filling the air around them. The sun had dipped below the horizon, casting the sky in shades of pink and purple, and there was a sense of peace and contentment between them, a feeling that they had found something truly special in each other.

They knew that their journey was far from over, that there would still be challenges and difficult moments ahead. But they also knew that they had the strength and the love to face them together. Their love had already changed them in so many ways, and they were confident that it would continue to do so, no matter what came their way.

Theological Reflection

LOVE IS THE MOST POWERFUL force in the universe, and it is eternal in nature. In 1 Corinthians 13:8, the Apostle Paul writes, "Love never fails. But where there are prophecies, they will cease; where there are tongues, they will be stilled; where there is knowledge, it will pass away." This verse reminds us that everything else in this world is temporary, but love—true, eternal love—never fails, never ends, and never passes away.

In the story of Grace and Ethan, we see the eternal nature of love at work in their lives. Their love has not only brought them together—it has connected them to something far greater than themselves, something eternal. It has given them a glimpse of the infinite, a reflection of God's love, and it has sustained them through every challenge and trial they have faced.

The eternal nature of love is not just about the here and now—it is about the promise of something greater, something that goes beyond time, something that connects us to God and to each other for eternity. It is about the way love transcends time, the way it continues to grow and flourish, even after we are gone. And it is about the way love changes us, heals us, and makes us into the best versions of ourselves.

As we reflect on the eternal nature of love, we are reminded that our ability to love is rooted in the love we have received from God. Just as God's love is eternal, unchanging, and infinite, so too are we called to love each other in a way that reflects that love, that connects us to something greater than ourselves, and that endures for all eternity.

May we always strive to love each other in a way that is powerful, that is transformative, that drives out fear and replaces it with peace and security. And may we find the strength to continue to grow, to continue to heal, to continue to love each other in a way that reflects the heart of God and the true power of love.

Chapter 15: The Promise of Everlasting Love

The late afternoon sun dipped low on the horizon, casting long shadows across the landscape and bathing everything in a warm, golden light. The world seemed to pause for a moment, as if holding its breath in reverence for the beauty of the fading day. In the distance, the soft sound of the ocean waves gently lapping against the shore could be heard, a soothing, rhythmic melody that had become a familiar part of their lives.

Grace Elliott and Ethan Matthews stood hand in hand at the edge of the cliff overlooking the ocean, their hearts full as they took in the breathtaking view before them. This was their favorite place, a secluded spot that had become their refuge, their sanctuary over the years. It was a place where they had shared their deepest thoughts, their hopes and dreams, their fears and doubts. It was a place where they had come to understand the true meaning of love, a love that had been tested and strengthened by time, a love that was grounded in their faith and the eternal promise of God's love.

As they stood there, side by side, the wind gently tousling their hair, Grace felt a deep sense of peace settle over her. She turned to look at Ethan, her heart swelling with love and gratitude for the man who had walked beside her through every season of life. His face was calm, his eyes filled with warmth and affection as he gazed out at the horizon. She could see the wisdom and experience etched into his features, the quiet strength that had been forged through years of faithfulness and love.

"I can't believe how far we've come," Grace said softly, her voice carrying a hint of awe. "It's hard to believe that we've been on this journey together for so long, that we've shared so much and grown so much together."

Ethan turned to her, a gentle smile playing on his lips. "It's been an incredible journey, hasn't it? We've faced so many challenges, so many trials, but through it all, we've held on to each other, and we've held on to our faith. I think that's what has brought us to this place, this place of peace and contentment."

Grace nodded, her heart filled with emotion. "I couldn't have done it without you, Ethan. You've been my rock, my constant source of strength and support. And I know that our love has been grounded in something so much greater than ourselves. It's been grounded in God's love, in the eternal promise of His love."

Ethan's smile deepened, and he gently squeezed her hand. "I've always believed that our love was a reflection of God's love, Grace. That it was a gift from Him, something that He has blessed and sustained through every season of our lives. And now, as we stand here, I can't help but feel overwhelmed by the depth of that love, by the promise of everlasting love that God has given us."

Grace felt tears well up in her eyes as she listened to his words, the truth of them resonating deep within her. "It's amazing, isn't it? How God's love is the foundation of everything, how it gives us the strength to face whatever comes our way, how it sustains us through the darkest of times. I think about Romans 8:38-39, where Paul writes, 'For I am convinced that neither death nor life... will be able to separate us from the love of God that is in Christ Jesus our Lord.' That promise is what has carried us through, what has kept us grounded in our faith and in each other."

Ethan nodded, his expression serious but filled with warmth. "It's a promise that we can hold on to, no matter what. The promise that God's love is everlasting, that it will never fail, never falter. It's a love that transcends everything—time, space, even death. And it's a love that has been the foundation of our relationship, the foundation of our lives."

Grace smiled through her tears, her heart overflowing with love and gratitude. "I'm so grateful for that promise, Ethan. I'm so grateful for the love that we've shared, for the life that we've built together. And I know that no matter what the future holds, our love will continue to endure, because it's grounded in something eternal, something everlasting."

They stood together in silence for a few moments, the sound of the waves and the rustling of the wind the only noises that filled the air. The sun had dipped even lower on the horizon, casting a golden glow over the ocean, and the sky was painted with shades of pink, orange, and purple. It was a breathtaking sight, one that seemed to mirror the beauty of the love they shared.

Finally, Ethan broke the silence, his voice soft and filled with emotion. "Grace, I want you to know that I am more convinced than ever that our love is something that will last forever. It's not just a love for this lifetime—it's a love that will continue on, even after we're gone. It's a love that is part of God's eternal plan, a love that is grounded in His everlasting promise."

Grace turned to look at him, her heart swelling with emotion. "I believe that too, Ethan. Our love is something that is so much bigger than ourselves, something that is part of God's greater plan. And I know that no matter what happens, no matter where life takes us, our love will endure, because it's grounded in God's love, in His promise of everlasting love."

Ethan smiled, his eyes filled with love and admiration. "I can't imagine my life without you, Grace. You've been my partner, my best friend, my greatest blessing. And I know that our love will continue to grow and flourish, because it's rooted in something eternal, something that will never fade or diminish."

Grace felt tears slip down her cheeks as she listened to his words, her heart overflowing with love and gratitude. "I feel the same way, Ethan. You've been my everything, the one who has stood by me through every challenge, every joy, every heartache. And I know that our love will continue to thrive, because it's grounded in God's everlasting love."

They stood together, hand in hand, as the sun dipped below the horizon, leaving the sky awash in a deep, rich blue. The stars began to twinkle above them, and the world seemed to be at peace, bathed in the soft glow of the moonlight.

As they stood there, Grace felt a deep sense of peace settle over her, a peace that came from knowing that their love was part of something so much greater than themselves, something eternal. It was a peace that came from knowing that they were connected to God, to each other, and to the promise of everlasting love that would carry them through this life and into the next.

IN THE DAYS AND WEEKS that followed, Grace and Ethan continued to reflect on the promise of everlasting love that had been the foundation of their relationship. They talked often about the ways their love had grown and deepened, about the ways it had connected them to each other and to God. They reflected on the journey they had been on together, the challenges they had faced, and the ways those challenges had strengthened their bond and made their love even more enduring.

One evening, as they sat together in their living room, the soft glow of the fireplace casting a warm light across the room, Grace turned to Ethan with a thoughtful expression. "I've been thinking a lot about what it means to love someone eternally," she began, her voice soft but filled with conviction. "About how our love isn't just for this lifetime—it's something that will last forever, something that will continue to grow and flourish, even after we're gone."

Ethan nodded, his gaze steady as he looked into her eyes. "I've been thinking about that too, Grace. And I think that's one of the most amazing things about love—how it has the power to transcend time, to connect us to something far greater than ourselves. It's like our love is a reflection of God's love, a small piece of something infinite and eternal."

Grace smiled, her heart swelling with love and gratitude. "It's such a comforting thought, isn't it? That no matter what happens, no matter what challenges we face, our love will endure. It's not just about this life—it's about something that goes beyond time, something that connects us to God and to each other for eternity."

Ethan's smile widened, his eyes twinkling with affection. "It is comforting. And it gives me so much peace to know that our love isn't just for this lifetime—it's something that will last forever, something that's part of God's eternal plan."

They sat together in comfortable silence, the warmth of their connection filling the air around them. The fire crackled softly in the fireplace, casting a gentle glow over the room, and there was a sense of peace and contentment between them, a feeling that they were exactly where they were meant to be.

AS THE YEARS PASSED, Grace and Ethan continued to experience the promise of everlasting love in their lives. They faced challenges and setbacks, moments of doubt and fear, but they always faced them together, always holding on to the love that had brought them together. Their love was not perfect—there were moments of frustration, moments of disagreement—but it was a love that had the power to change, to heal, to make them into the best versions of themselves.

One evening, as they sat together on the porch, watching the sun set over the city, Grace turned to Ethan with a smile. "I've been thinking a lot about our journey," she began, her voice soft but filled with emotion. "About everything we've been through, and how much we've changed, how much we've grown together."

Ethan nodded, his expression thoughtful. "I've been thinking about that too, Grace. I think that's one of the most amazing things about love—how it has the power to change us, to heal us, to make us into the best versions of ourselves. I've seen that in you, in us, and I'm so grateful for it."

Grace smiled, her heart swelling with love and gratitude for the man beside her. "I'm so grateful for that too, Ethan. I'm so grateful for you, for the love we share. I believe that our love has the power to continue to change us, to continue to heal us, to make us stronger, no matter what comes our way."

Ethan reached out and took her hand, his voice filled with warmth and affection. "I believe that too, Grace. And I'm committed to continuing to show you the power of love, every single day. I know that as long as we keep making that choice, our love will continue to grow, to heal, to transform us."

They sat together in comfortable silence, the warmth of their connection filling the air around them. The sun had dipped below the horizon, casting the sky in shades of pink and purple, and there was a sense of peace and contentment between them, a feeling that they had found something truly special in each other.

They knew that their journey was far from over, that there would still be challenges and difficult moments ahead. But they also knew that they had the strength and the love to face them together. Their love had already changed them in so many ways, and they were confident that it would continue to do so, no matter what came their way.

Theological Reflection

THE PROMISE OF EVERLASTING love is the cornerstone of the Christian faith. In Romans 8:38-39, the Apostle Paul writes, "For I am convinced that neither death nor life, neither angels nor demons, neither the present nor the future, nor any powers, neither height nor depth, nor anything else in all creation, will be able to separate us from the love of God that is in Christ Jesus our Lord." This verse reminds us that God's love is everlasting, unchanging, and infinite. It is a love that transcends time, space, and even death. It is a love that connects us to God and to each other for eternity.

In the story of Grace and Ethan, we see the power of everlasting love at work in their lives. Their love has not only brought them together—it has connected them to something far greater than themselves, something eternal. It has given them a glimpse of the infinite, a reflection of God's love, and it has sustained them through every challenge and trial they have faced.

The promise of everlasting love is not just about the here and now—it is about the future, about the promise of something greater, something that goes beyond time, something that connects us to God and to each other for eternity. It is about the way love transcends time, the way it continues to grow and flourish, even after we are gone. And it is about the way love changes us, heals us, and makes us into the best versions of ourselves.

As we reflect on the promise of everlasting love, we are reminded that our ability to experience that love is rooted in the love we have received from God. Just as God's love is eternal, unchanging, and infinite, so too are we called to love each other in a way that reflects that love, that connects us to something greater than ourselves, and that endures for all eternity.

May we always strive to love each other in a way that is powerful, that is transformative, that drives out fear and replaces it with peace and security. And may we find the strength to continue to grow, to continue to heal, to continue to love each other in a way that reflects the heart of God and the true power of everlasting love.

Don't miss out!

Visit the website below and you can sign up to receive emails whenever Angela Marie Stewart publishes a new book. There's no charge and no obligation.

https://books2read.com/r/B-A-LZEHC-EGAZE

BOOKS 2 READ

Connecting independent readers to independent writers.

Did you love *Love's True Promise*? Then you should read *Faithful Love*[1] by Angela Marie Stewart!

"**Faithful Love**" delves into the profound connection between faith and love, offering a comprehensive exploration of how these two forces shape and sustain romantic relationships. Through theological reflections, scriptural insights, and practical applications, each chapter guides readers on a journey of understanding love's foundation, its endurance through trials, and its ultimate expression as a reflection of God's eternal covenant with humanity. This book is an inspiring resource for couples seeking to deepen their spiritual and emotional bond, anchored in the timeless truths of scripture.

---

1. https://books2read.com/u/mdEROd

2. https://books2read.com/u/mdEROd

About the Author

Angela Marie Stewart is a cherished author known for her heartfelt Christian romance fiction. With a passion for weaving tales that inspire faith and love, Angela's novels explore the transformative power of grace and the enduring strength of the human spirit. Her writing journey reflects her deep commitment to portraying love stories grounded in Christian values and spiritual growth. Angela's work resonates with readers seeking uplifting narratives and the comfort of faith intertwined with romance. When she's not writing, Angela enjoys community service, spending time with her family, and exploring the beauty of her surroundings.